COLORADO GOLD DUST

Short Stories and Profiles

by

Dave Southworth

Wild Horse Publishing

Contents

PREFACE 5

TRAIL OF THE SEVEN MATCHES 7

COLORFUL KINGPIN SOAPY SMITH 11

JOHN DUGAN, OF FRAIL MIND 15

THE LYNCHINGS - A TURN OF FAIRPLAY 17

BABY DOE AND THE TABOR TRIANGLE 19

PAT CASEY'S NIGHT HANDS 23

FIRE AND BRIMSTONE 25

THE HATFIELD STORY 31

SOILED DOVES OF BLAIR STREET 33

COLORADO'S ONLY SUBMARINE 41

THE REFORMATION OF COCKEYED LIZ 43

VOYAGE BEYOND THE BLUE 47

CLARA BROWN, PIONEER 51

COLORADO'S OTHER CAPITOL CITY 55

TIN CUP BLOOD 59

OH BE JOYFUL'S RESCUE 61

BUCK ROGERS' LOST GOLD MINE 63

THE LITTLE MAN WHO MOVED MOUNTAINS 65

THE GREAT ICE PALACE 69

NO READIN', WRITIN', OR 'RITHMETIC 73

SILVERHEELS 75

THE BACA GRANT: ITS EFFECT ON
    AREA MINING SETTLEMENTS 79

HOW BRECKENRIDGE GOT ITS NAME 83

SPORTS AND RECREATION IN "THE WORLDS
    GREATEST GOLD CAMP" 85

BROKEN NOSE SCOTTY 89

LOST BROTHER - LOST GOLD 91

GUNFIGHTS ON GREENE STREET 95

THOMAS WALSH AND THE CAMPBIRD 99

TO HELL YOU RIDE 103

CAVERNA DEL ORO 109

BIRD ON A MOUNTAIN TOP 113

SWINDLE AT PERU 115

LEADVILLE: HOW IT HAPPENED 117

THE PELICAN AND DIVES' FEUD 125

FOILED FLIGHT 129

CANNIBAL PACKER 131

RED LIGHTS OF MYERS AVENUE 135

THE VICTOR LABOR WARS 139

PRUNES, A BURRO 143

POOR JAMES FENTON 145

THE MEEKER MASSACRE 147

GOOD GUYS AND BAD GUYS 149

BACHELOR'S SAD STORY 151

ASPEN, THE EARLY YEARS 153

JOHN OSGOOD'S UTOPIA 159

EAT, DRINK AND BE MERRY 161

THE ILL-FATED JIM REYNOLD'S GANG 163

THE UNSINKABLE MRS. BROWN 165

ACKNOWLEDGEMENTS 169

BIBLIOGRAPHY 171

Preface

Following the discovery of gold by William Green Russell at Dry Creek in 1858, hundreds of prospectors swarmed to the camps of Denver City and Auraria. The Pike's Peak gold rush was on. Miners combed the hills but found very little to show for it. Most left in disgust. The grumbles, however, soon turned to cheers. In the spring of 1859, George Jackson and John Gregory made rich gold strikes near Idaho Springs and Central City respectively. This time thousands came. Other discoveries soon followed, and mining camps cropped up throughout the mountains. Fortune seekers headed west with whatever belongings they could stuff into a satchel or wagon.

When a mining camp showed promise, its tents were replaced by log cabins. As communities grew and sawmills were erected, frame structures were built. Stores were usually erected side-by-side with imposing false fronts hiding the buildings behind them.

In the early 1860s the most common form of mining was placering. Prospectors combed mountain streams in search of promising color. Others looked for exposed ore or float gold. Before long, the easily obtainable gold had been found, and miners began sinking shafts into the mountainsides. When silver was discovered in 1877, another boom followed. Soon there was more silver produced than gold in Colorado. Mining efficiency and the population explosion were both aided by a new maze of railroads which snaked their way through valleys and over mountain passes.

At first, men outnumbered women by a margin of thirty to one. Brothels and dance halls sprang up in every mining camp for the entertainment of the miners. Some camps had more saloons than bunkhouses. In fact, some saloons were bunkhouses. At a certain hour the bar would close and bedrolls would cover the floor. Gamblers and prostitutes were quick to fleece a miner of his gold dust. In most communities there was little or no law. Fisticuffs and gunfights were common. The early mining settlements had a reputation for being tough and rowdy. Each community, it seems, was a melting pot of very different people -- from very different backgrounds -- each trying to get rich off the mountains or off others who had already struck paydirt. Each community had its colorful characters as well. There were gamblers and con artists, tin stars and gunslingers, itinerant preachers and parlor girls, paupers and millionaires, heros and heroines, thieves and cowards, dreamers and fools. There were many characters who created great legends.

A legend might be authentic history which has grown in stature over the years. It can also be an unauthentic story handed down by tradition and popularly regarded as historical. The stories and profiles in this book are probably a little of both. They include this writer's versions of some often-told stories, others rarely heard, and profiles of some fascinating people and places. A few selected passages (some which are abridged) have been extracted from this writer's other works.

Each night Jones would scatter his matches

TRAIL OF THE SEVEN MATCHES

Prospector Marc Jones was very superstitious. He believed that when a handful of wooden matches was scattered, if seven match heads ever pointed in one direction, a rich vein could be found along that line.

Jones and his partners, Heon Hastings and John Anson, had been mining for some time west of Leadville on Sugar Loaf Mountain. All of their ore was low-grade, but their hopes remained high. They were certain that one day they would strike it rich. Each night when the trio returned to their cabin, Jones would scatter his matches on the table. There were times when as many as six match heads pointed in one direction, but six wasn't enough.

Then one day it happened. He tossed the matches and seven lined up perfectly parallel with their heads pointing south toward Mount Elbert. The following morning Jones packed up to follow his strange compass. He asked his partners to travel with him, but Hastings and Anson would have none of his foolishness.

Several days went by before the hungry and bedraggled Jones returned. Hastings and Anson had never seen such a broad grin on his face. Jones pulled a handful of yellow nuggets from his pocket. He also brought back two sacks of dirt which had the best gold content the trio had ever seen.

Jones told his partners how he followed the seven matches which led him up a narrow canyon, through a wide gorge, and on to a high-mountain meadow. On a hillside beside the meadow, Jones found the ruins of an old tunnel. Some timbers had fallen and were blocking the entrance to the old mine. Jones was certain that the seven matches had led him to this spot. It took him a full day of clearing before he could enter the mine. Jones further explained that he could pick up the plentiful samples at random, and that he believed he had found a bonanza.

Anson and Hastings accompanied Jones to Leadville to have the samples assayed. The tests showed the ore to be rich in gold content. The assayer filled out a card which contained the date, June 2, 1882, Marc Jones' name, the test results, and the name of the mine -- the South Paw Mine. When asked how he arrived at the name, Jones explained that his left hand was the best friend he ever had -- that it had provided for him all his life -- so he named the old mine after his best friend.

Shortly thereafter, Jones, Hastings and Anson packed up and set out for the South Paw. The trio followed the course that Jones had originally taken, as dictated by the seven matches. Once again, Jones reached the narrow canyon, this time with his partners following. Suddenly there was a small rock slide above. Jones was struck on the head and knocked unconscious.

When Marc Jones finally regained consciousness -- he didn't know his friends -- he didn't know anything about the South Paw Mine -- in fact, he didn't know anything about mining. The injury had caused amnesia.

Marc Jones' memory never returned, and he died without being able to tell anyone the location of the South Paw. Heon Hastings and John Anson spent the next six years searching for the mine -- but never found it.

Jefferson Randolph Smith

COLORFUL KINGPIN SOAPY SMITH

Jefferson Randolph Smith followed the carnival into booming Leadville, Colorado, in the early '80s. He was learning the art of "sleight of hand," the old shell game, and other slick tricks designed to milk a man of his hard-earned money. He learned well from the carnival pros, but the con game that intrigued him the most was run by a fellow named Taylor, on the corner of Third Street and Madison Avenue. Taylor's game was to wrap ten, twenty or fifty dollar bills around cakes of soap which were rewrapped in their blue squares and shuffled into a large pile of identically wrapped cakes. He then offered the crowd their choice for five dollars. A shill would be the first to try. Naturally, he would find a larger bill wrapped around

11

his soap cake, and would holler with glee. Enthralled by the con game and amazed at how much money Taylor could make, Jeff Smith wanted to learn more. So, he went to work for Taylor as a shill.

Soon thereafter, Smith arrived in Denver and set up his own soap scam near Union Station. He grew a beard to disguise his youthfulness, and became very adroit at his game. It was during this time that Smith earned the nickname "Soapy."

Soapy Smith could handle a deck of cards as well, and soon added gambling to his repertoire. He trained others to be con artists, then put them to work for a piece of their action. He hired some toughs to handle the objections of those who were rooked, and to double as bodyguards. Before long he had a gang in place -- a gang which was influential and powerful. In order to operate his cons effectively, Soapy set up an office at Seventeenth and Larimer streets.

One incident in Denver probably added more to Soapy's notoriety than any other thing. After reading in the newspaper that the Glasson Detective Agency had attempted to force a confession from a pretty little girl, Soapy went into action. Soapy invaded the Glasson offices with pistols blaring. He shot the place up and generally made a shambles of everything. He let it be known that under no circumstances would anyone mistreat a little girl like that. Soapy Smith became a hero in Denver.

Soapy married an attractive lady from St. Louis. The couple had three children. Although he provided well for his family, Soapy wasn't much of a family man. His mob came first. Denver soon grew tired of his shady activities, and Soapy looked for new fields to conquer.

The year 1892 brought one of the great booms in Colorado history -- at Creede. Silver strikes brought people at the rate of nearly 300 per day. There was no law -- there was no government. Saloons and gambling halls popped up everywhere. The camp had a carnival-like atmosphere. Soapy wanted part of the action and moved to Creede.

With his old friend Joe Simmons, Soapy built the Orleans Club which he also established as his headquarters. Soapy's notoriety from Denver preceded him, and he was welcomed into Creede as a celebrity. With part of his Denver gang at his side, he quickly set up a dictatorship and ruled Creede. The only rival Soapy had was Bob Ford -- the man who killed Jesse James. Ford owned a dance hall and saloon called the Exchange. Ford finally acknowledged Soapy's superiority, but it didn't matter for long. In June 1892, Bob Ford was shot and killed by Ed O'Kelley in the same manner in which Ford had killed Jesse James -- in the back. "Soapy's government" wasn't bad. For the most part, he and his gang maintained law and order. Troublemakers were run out of town.

Unaware of Soapy Smith's control over the community, a brash young gambler known as the New Orleans Kid, arrived in Creede. He set up a shell game in front of the Orleans Club. Soapy ordered him to leave, but the kid wouldn't budge. Furthermore he stated that he would gun down Soapy Smith or any of his gang members who got in his way. Late that night, Joe Palmer one of Soapy's men, stepped outside the Orleans Club. The kid drew and shot off one of Palmer's thumbs. Shots were fired in each direction and both men were wounded. The New Orleans Kid hobbled out of Creede, knowing that he would be more welcome in another town.

Parson Uzzell, from Central City, arrived in town to preach at the dedication of a gospel tent. After taking up a collection, Parson Uzzell had his pants and the contributions stolen. Soapy immediately saw to it that the parson's trousers and money were returned -- with the kitty slightly fattened. On another occasion, a minister was attempting to collect funds for a new church. The crowd which had gathered was disrespectful and noisy.

Soapy stepped in and within about two hours had collected $600 to the disbelief of the parson. After the church was constructed, Soapy and some of his gang attended the first service.

An imaginative fellow by the name of Bob Fitzsimmons cast a human-like cement body over some skeletal remains. He perpetrated a hoax by digging the "petrified" man out of a mud bank -- then brought his great discovery to Creede. Realizing that something was fishy, and quick to capitalize on the matter, Soapy purchased the petrified creature. The seven-foot tall man of stone was dubbed "McGinty," and set up at the Orleans Club as the silver camp's greatest attraction. After everybody had paid at least once to see the petrified man, Soapy leased the critter out to a traveling circus.

As the citizens of Creede began to establish a stable government, Soapy began to lose his grasp. Once more it was time to move on -- and so he did, to Skagway, Alaska. Skagway was another boom town, ripe for his pickings. For a while he ruled Skagway in the same manner in which he had ruled Creede. On July 8, 1898, in a gunfight with a fellow named Frank Reid, Soapy Smith lost his life.

He just drifted along as though he owned the earth

JOHN DUGAN, OF FRAIL MIND

John Dugan was better known as "Rain-in-the-Face," although nobody is totally sure why. He was a plain, honest, harmless, simple-minded old soul -- with an emphasis on simple-minded. Everybody loved him, and he loved everybody.

Dugan was a hard-working prospector who spent all his time looking for the pot at the end of the rainbow. Age was upon him and his constitution reflected the years of continuous toil. John Dugan arrived in Rico in 1888. He spent most of each year in the nearby hills with his pick and shovel. Each winter he rolled his blankets and walked over several mountains to spend the winters at Durango where the climate was more stable, but he always returned to Rico in the early spring.

Before coming to Rico, the beloved old soul spent fourteen years in Arkansas, digging in an orchard for hidden treasure. He never found any and finally decided to move on.

"Rain-in-the-Face" spent most of '90 and '91 driving a tunnel into the south hillside in Aztec Gulch -- supposedly in search of a hidden treasure vault of ore. It is said that Dugan staked his claim on another man's location. Should he have found a bonanza, he would have toiled in vain for his rewards would have belonged to another.

Of pleasant disposition and frail mind, friendly old John Dugan just drifted along as though he owned the earth. It is much better to labor in poverty and be content, than to be heavy in riches and discontent.

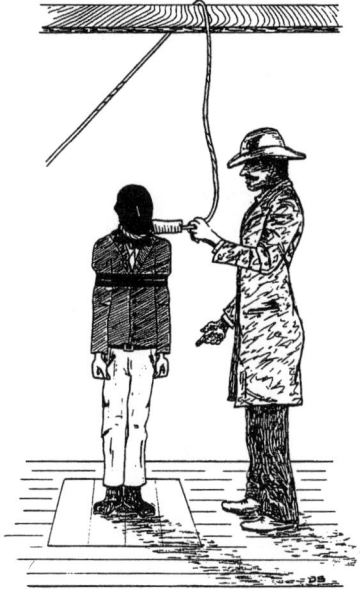

Simms claimed he was too light to be hanged

THE LYNCHINGS - A TURN OF FAIRPLAY

Fairplay's fateful "Tuesday Murder" occurred on April 3, 1879. The Bergh House (now the Fairplay Hotel) hired a fellow named Thomas M. Bennett to work on a drainage ditch that ran down the street in front of the hotel. John J. Hoover was upset over the progress being made on the ditch which also passed in front of his billiard parlor. He had a drink or two then walked into the hotel lobby, found Bennett, uttered a few ornery words and shot him dead. Hoover was jailed, tried, and sentenced to eight years in prison by Judge Thomas Bowen. Enraged by the light sentence, the citizens took the law into their own hands. They broke Hoover out of jail and hanged him from the second-

17

story window of the Court House until he was dead.

When Judge Bowen arrived at the Court House the following morning, he found a noosed rope across his bench. Nearby, was a second rope tagged "for the district attorney." The message was well received, as both the judge and district attorney quickly left town in a cloud of dust.

In another incident, a drunken fellow named Sam Porter staggered on to the street bragging that he would kill the first man he saw. Unaware of the danger, John Carmody approached the drunk. Porter aimed, shot, and killed Carmody instantly. Once again the town's citizens took matters into their own hands. On the exterior wall of the jail they nailed a strut, then tossed a noose over it. They slipped the noose around Porter's neck, and asked him if he had any last words. "Yes," he answered, "Pull!"

Fairplay's first official public hanging occurred on July 19, 1880. Cicero Simms killed John Johnson in a local barroom, after it appeared to witnesses that they were simply having an innocent spat. Johnson, who was respected and well-liked in the community, had been providing room and board for Simms. While awaiting trial for murder, Simms, who was a skinny lad, boasted that he was too light to be hanged. He was found guilty and sentenced to death by hanging. To avoid trouble during the ordeal, Simms' two brothers were temporarily locked up in jail. Eight hundred people, including many ladies, watched as Simms climbed on to the newly constructed gallows. His face was covered, and the noose was slipped around his neck. The trapdoor dropped and Simms hung motionless.

Simms' brothers were released from jail and took custody of the body. According to one story, a stagecoach driver was stopped that evening by two men who had an injured companion. The driver, who was forced to take the three to Leadville at gunpoint, later identified the injured man as Cicero Simms.

18

Elizabeth "Baby Doe" Tabor

BABY DOE AND THE TABOR TRIANGLE

Among the earliest arrivals into California Gulch during the spring of 1860, were Horace Austin Warner Tabor and his wife Augusta. H.A.W. Tabor, who was to become a pillar in the development of Leadville, arrived during a food shortage. He sacrificed his oxen so that hungry miners could eat, and by doing so immediately became the friend of many. Augusta established a little store where she sold her baked goods and provided meals as well. Like most of the men, Horace prospected the surrounding hills.

In May 1878, Horace Tabor grubstaked August Rische and George Hook to $17 worth of supplies for a third interest in their findings. He added another $47 worth of tools to the grubstake. Rische and Hook discovered the Little Pittsburg (often spelled Pittsburgh) Mine and made Tabor an instant millionaire. Tabor once purchased a "salted" mine, the Chrysolite, for $900 from a swindler named "Chicken Bill" Lovell. Instead of considering it a bad deal, he further developed the property and struck rich silver ore which reaped a bonanza of $3,000,000. Later, Tabor purchased the Matchless Mine for $117,000 -- possibly the only investment he made without partners. During the peak years of its operation, the Matchless yielded $1,000,000 per year.

Augusta Tabor was accustomed to a modest lifestyle and did not agree with the lavish tastes that accompanied Horace's newfound fortune. He spent or gave away his money almost as fast as he received it. Horace and Augusta drew further apart. It wasn't long before the beautiful divorcee, Elizabeth McCourt Doe, caught his eye.

Attractive and vivacious Lizzie McCourt loved to ice skate and also had visions of one day becoming a great actress. In Oshkosh, Wisconsin, on June 27, 1877, she married shy, but dignified, William Harvey Doe, Jr.. Immediately thereafter the couple departed for Central City, Colorado where Harvey's father, Colonel W.H. Doe, Sr. had mining interests. Harvey was to work Colonel Doe's share of the Fourth of July Mine for its profits, with the stipulation that if he was successful the share would be deeded to the newlyweds in a year. Lizzie dreamed of riches. Luck wasn't on their side, however, for the mine failed to produce high-grade ore and their capital was running very low. The couple moved to a small, second story, two room apartment in Black Hawk in order to save money. Dissention set in -- and it soon turned to quarreling. Their debts increased and Harvey became irresponsible. Disillusioned, and seeking excitement, Lizzie began hanging out at Central City's flashy variety hall, the Shoo-fly. To the miners and sporting girls Lizzie became known as Baby Doe. Naturally she heard all the talk around the Shoo-fly, and elsewhere, about the meteoric rise of silver and the new fortune of Horace Tabor.

Harvey had deserted Baby Doe while she was pregnant. Then she gave birth to a still-born baby. A friend, Jake Sandelowsky, who later shortened his name to Sands, sent the discouraged Baby Doe to Leadville for a "change of scenery." During her visit, Baby Doe heard more and more about Leadville's number one citizen, H.A.W. Tabor. Baby Doe divorced Harvey on March 19, 1880, then moved to Leadville. She dreamed of the day she might meet Horace Tabor -- and finally she did.

Instantly, there was magic when the two met at the Saddle Rock Cafe. Before the evening was over Tabor had written a check to the awe-struck Baby Doe for $5,000. Within days he had moved her into a suite at the Clarendon Hotel, and they became lovers.

As Lieutenant Governor of Colorado, Horace and his wife Augusta entertained society in their fine house in Denver. His visits to Leadville were frequent, however, and he spent much time with Baby Doe -- and people talked. Later, Horace moved Baby Doe into a plush suite at the elegant Windsor Hotel in Denver.

Augusta was a plain and simple woman who became increasingly more critical of Horace's extravagant way of life as well as his politics. Horace asked her for a divorce, but she refused. When Augusta was absent at the festive opening of the Tabor Grand Opera House (September 5, 1881), there were more whispers.

Eventually, in a surprise move, Augusta filed a suit for property settlement, asking Tabor for $50,000 per year and their Denver home. Tabor had the suit suppressed for being without the jurisdiction of the court. Meanwhile, Horace obtained a "secret" divorce in Durango, where he was a property owner and had a friend who was a judge. There was a question in Horace's mind as to the validity of what he had just done. In the developments which followed, Augusta sued for divorce and received a settlement of mining stock, their Denver house, and other real estate. Horace accepted an appointment to fill the thirty days remaining on the senatorial term of Henry M. Teller.

These events paved the way for the lavish wedding of Horace and Baby Doe. They were married March 1, 1883, in Washington D.C. with many dignitaries in attendance -- including President Chester Arthur. Unlike the first Mrs. Tabor, Baby Doe was extravagant and helped Horace spend his money. The couple lived in grand style for ten years during which time Horace and Baby Doe gave birth to three children. Elizabeth Bonduel Lillie was born July 13, 1884. On October 17, 1888, Baby Doe gave birth to a son who lived only a few hours. Another daughter, Rose Mary Echo Silver Dollar was born December 17, 1889. Baby Doe bought thousand-dollar dresses for her daughters. The fairytale life, however, was to end.

The silver crash of 1893 depleted the fortune of H.A.W. Tabor. The man who had been mayor of Leadville, Lieutenant Governor of Colorado, and briefly a U.S. Senator, died a pauper in 1899. Baby Doe's devotion to Horace was unwavering, even through the tough years. Augusta had always believed that one day Horace would come back to her, but it was not to be for he and Baby Doe remained totally loyal to each other until his death. Abandoned by both her daughters, Baby Doe spent her remaining years living in the small shack adjacent to the Matchless Mine, until her frozen body was found one day in 1935. Seldom has anyone experienced such contrasts in beauty and decay or wealth and poverty.

Out for a Sunday drive

PAT CASEY'S NIGHT HANDS

Pat Casey was an unmarried Irishman who loved women -- but he wasn't very bright. It wasn't because he loved women, mind you, he just didn't have a formal education. Like most Irishmen, Casey also loved his whiskey. The problem was, Casey couldn't afford either -- the women or the whiskey.

One day while digging a grave outside of Central City, Casey struck gold. He filed a claim and called it the Casey Mine. All of a sudden Casey was rich -- and all of a sudden he could afford women and whiskey. He quickly made up for lost time. He surrounded himself with bodyguards -- a group of barfly friends whom he called his "night hands." The time that he didn't spend in the saloons he spent in the brothels, and, he frequented them regularly. In fact, he spent so much time with "sporting girls" that he was shunned by the town ladies and frowned upon for his activities. Casey didn't mind, for he had all the girls money could buy. Everything was going his way -- he even had a street named after him.

Legend has it that Casey would rent a fancy carriage on Sundays, pick up the "hurdy gurdy girls," and ride past the community churches just so he could see the town ladies in a huff. Casey and the girls would strut, while the ladies turned their noses in the air.

The Casey Mine poured forth riches, and Pat Casey spent them as fast as he could. He became a natty dresser with a stylish wardrobe. He upgraded his taste to champagne and showered his favorite girls with fancy gifts.

"What a colorful character to present on stage," thought Mike Dougherty -- so, he penned *Pat Casey's Night Hands*. The first show was scheduled to open April 27, 1863, in Mountain City's Montana Theatre, with Jack S. Langrishe and his local players performing the spoof.

When Pat Casey first heard about the production, he was outraged. Nobody was going to stage a public mockery of Pat Casey if he could help it. Intent on ruining the performance, he bought tickets for his "night hands" and all the other toughs he could find. When they heard of the potential trouble, Dougherty and Langrishe hired armed guards who were also in attendance. The show went on. No disturbance occurred, and Pat Casey laughed as jauntily as anybody.

Life went on. The following Sunday, Casey was probably in a fancy carriage again with his "hurdy gurdy girls," making the rounds of the churches to see whose dander he could raise.

Father John L. Dyer

FIRE AND BRIMSTONE

The Lord must have looked down into the Colorado mining camps and said, "My oh my, those hardworking souls seem to spend every leisure minute in saloons, gambling halls, and bordellos. We need to send help." And so he did. A few men of the cloth ventured into Colorado, hoping to bring a little religion to the rough and tough mining camps. They preached in saloons, dance halls, on the streets, or wherever they could gather a crowd.

Father John L. Dyer was a Methodist layman. He wasn't an ordained minister, but he felt the call to preach. Father Dyer, who was possibly the first to preach in a Colorado mining camp, wandered into Buckskin Joe in 1861 with little more than a prayer book to his name. In this predominantly God-forsaken country, he spread the gospel wherever he could find a few men gathered together -- whether in a gambling hall or a mine. Dyer was a dedicated missionary who covered most of the mining camps in the area that now includes Park, Lake, and Summit counties. And, he did so afoot. During the winters he traveled on skis -- over ten feet long (in those days they were called snow-shoes). His collections were meager, so he worked odd jobs to help pay expenses. He carried mail, hauled bags of gold dust, and even drove a stage for a while so he could continue to spread the word of God.

The snow-shoe itinerant mixed a little prospecting with his preaching, especially during his later years. He staked the Warrior's Mark Mine near the summit of Boreas Pass. Nearby he built a cabin in the place later known as Dyersville. For his interest in the mine, Father Dyer (who was always broke) ended up with about $2,000.

Another Methodist was pistol-toting Big John Chivington. With his large stature and deep voice, he commanded an audience. When he walked into a saloon and declared that he was going to preach, everybody listened. Chivington later became more renowned as commander of Colorado's Third Regiment which slaughtered Black Kettle and the Cheyennes in the Sand Creek Massacre. Black Kettle flew the American flag and a white flag on the same staff, but they were ignored by Chivington.

Father Joseph P. Macheboeuf spread Catholicism to mining camps near and far. He was a man of small stature, with a big heart, and the stamina to work at an untiring pace. "I thank God that I have more work than I can do," he often said. He traveled the rough trails between mining camps in a small buggy which contained a portable altar. Father Joseph P. Macheboeuf held Catholic services most anywhere he could find space, including a billiard room. In Central City, one Sunday, frustrated with the situation, he locked the doors and wouldn't allow his congregation to leave until they had pledged enough money to build a new Catholic Church. The French priest, who had all of Colorado and Utah as a diocese, later became Bishop Macheboeuf.

The Reverend Sheldon Jackson, pioneer for the Presbyterian Church, was in charge of missionary work in most of the western territories. Wherever he spread the gospel, Jackson would leave posted notices stating, "Presbyterians moving west will please leave their names and destination with the Reverend Sheldon Jackson, so that they may be looked after and church privileges supplied them as early as possible." Only one Presbyterian registered. The Sheldon Jackson Memorial Chapel at Fairplay is a tribute to the man whose missionary work covered a vast area of the west.

Father Robinson, of Fairplay, often crossed Mosquito Pass to preach in California Gulch. Later, during the silver boom in 1878, he established the first place of worship in Leadville.

The "Fighting Parson", Reverend Tom A. Uzzell, also spent much time in Leadville. Parson Uzzell preached in barns and saloons while raising funds for a church building. He also had a "claim" on a lot on which to construct the church. One day some "claim jumpers" were preparing the lot for mining. Parson Uzzell stripped off his coat and waded into the miners. Later he said, "I made up my mind if the Lord wanted me to recover that lot He would give me strength to lick those fellows -- and He did." On another occasion, Uzzell was asked to speak at a funeral for a less-than-reputable member of the community. Gamblers, prostitutes, and saloonkeepers were in attendance. After the internment, Uzzell was told, "You gave us hell, but I guess we deserved it. Here's fifty dollars."

Parson Uzzell crossed paths with con man Soapy Smith on several occasions. One time while in the rowdy mining camp of Creede, a collection was taken up while Uzzell stood on a pool table and preached. Later that night his pants and the collection were stolen. Soapy Smith found the culprit and ordered him to return the trousers with additional money, over and above the collection. On another occasion in Denver, Smith helped Parson Uzzell provide a fine Christmas dinner for the poor by donating $1,500 of his faro winnings to the cause.

The Reverend Joseph Gaston, a pastor from Ouray, once received permission from a Creede gambling hall to preach for fifteen minutes. Gaston climbed on the faro dealer's chair and led three hundred men in the recitation of the Lord's Prayer.

In 1891 the Reverend William Davis was sent by the Congregational Church to Red Mountain in order to establish a mission. The pastor received a polite but cool reception. Finding no place in which to conduct worship services, he went to Guston where he was cordially received. More determined than ever, Davis set out to raise money for construction of a church. Contributions were received from Silverton to Ouray, the land and pews were donated, and the little church became a reality. Somebody suggested that a mine whistle should be installed in the belfry in order to be heard near and far. Reverend Davis thought that to be a marvelous idea -- and so it was. It is the only church known to have announced its services with the shrill blast of a whistle.

Lake City had a wild red-light district. In Hell's Acre, as it was called, gambling dens and dance halls were mixed with many brothels. The community had a legendary preacher, Reverend George M. Darley, who documented his experiences. He was another who preached the gospel in the most unlikely places. Darley believed that the folks who needed religion the most were the ones who lived in, and frequented, Hell's Acre, so he spread the holy word in gambling dens and dance halls.

There were many preachers who wandered around the mountains during the early years. As communities became

28

established -- so did the preachers. Hell-fire and damnation were heard in the strangest places. Some people must have listened, for they eventually built churches.

Lillian Hatfield loved music

THE HATFIELD STORY

Gold was discovered in the 1880s in Black Canyon, Jenny Lind Gulch, and on Baltimore Ridge. Many other discoveries followed and the area began to boom. The settlement of Black Canyon served the miners and mines in the Phoenix District. The name of the town was changed in 1896 to Baltimore. A post office was established that same year, and John Hatfield was named postmaster. Hatfield was quite instrumental in the development of Baltimore. He owned many mining claims and was the original owner of the town site itself.

John Hatfield was born July 4, 1854, in the Big Thompson Canyon area, placing him among the earliest Colorado natives. Hatfield once claimed that he received an award from the

Denver Post for being Colorado's oldest native resident.

Amidst many cabins, a dance hall, drugstore, and saloon (the famous Baltimore Club) were constructed. Because the sale of liquor was prohibited in nearby Tolland (Mammoth), the Baltimore Club flourished. And it did so right on into the days of Prohibition, because Hatfield simply ignored the law. When law enforcement officers carried Hatfield and his whiskey to Central City, the evidence quickly evaporated as it had a wondrous taste. The officers had to release Hatfield for "lack of evidence."

Lillian Woodard was born July 5, 1868. She was a composer and an accomplished pianist who had studied at the Boston Conservatory of Music. In 1905, she became Mrs. John Hatfield. Soon a piano arrived in Baltimore -- later, a wagonload of curtains. The dance hall was converted into an opera house. Lillian was talented and sophisticated. John, though stubborn, was bright and enterprising. The couple loved to entertain. People came from near and far to enjoy their marvelous hospitality. On the road from Rollinsville to Tolland, at the cut-off to Baltimore, John Hatfield erected a sign which read, "Baltimore -- shortcut to Apex and Central City," which then was followed by a list of the town's amenities. Lillian staged many musicals at the opera house over the ensuing years. John built several cabins to use as tourist rentals. Each had names such as, "Bluebell," or "Jewel," etc. They had grandiose plans of building Baltimore into a superior resort. Their dreams, however, never materialized.

Lillian Hatfield may have gone overboard "entertaining." The dressing rooms on the second floor of the opera house were converted (it is rumored) into a brothel. John operated several stills to keep his good whiskey flowing at the Baltimore Club.

Lillian's piano still sits inside the log house "Sunbeam," once the Hatfield home. Directly across the street the Baltimore Club stands precariously -- propped by large timbers.

The Mikado

SOILED DOVES OF BLAIR STREET

Silverton's Blair Street was one of Colorado's most notorious red-light districts. It was lined with saloons, dance halls, gambling dens, elegant bordellos, and seedy cribs -- and it operated "wide open" twenty-four hours a day. Alice Morris purchased the first building to be actually used as a brothel in 1878. "Jew" Fanny was the last prostitute to openly pedal her wares. She left Silverton when the Shenandoah-Dives Mine closed in 1952. During the interim there were about seventy-five years of, "there'll be a hot time in the old town tonight." Most of it happened on Blair Street.

William and Jane Bowen built and operated the Westminster Hall on Greene Street. William fell into poor health and deeded all of his property to Jane. Jane then purchased the lot directly behind Westminster Hall upon which she constructed a new dance hall, which faced Blair Street. Jane Bowen's Dance Hall became the first large bordello in Silverton. Many more were to follow.

The June 16, 1883, edition of the *Silverton Democrat* reported:

> "Considerable interest has been taken in the action of the Grand Jury, which brought in 117 indictments against lewd women ... Upon each and every prostitute, a fine of five dollars and costs were imposed."

Most of the girls operated on Blair Street -- and business was booming.

There are many stories to tell about Blair Street -- and its colorful residents. Most of the girls seemed to gain their notoriety from violent or lawless acts which received attention in the local newspapers. Molly Foley arrived in Silverton in 1878. She was a "seasoned" prostitute who had previously "worked" other western settlements. On Blair Street she established a small den and assumed the role as madame. The following is a vivid account of a fist fight as described by the *San Juan Democrat*:

> "Two fair but frail maidens of Blair Street fame, sailing under the euphonious titles of Molly Foley and Lizzie Fisher, had a slight altercation last Saturday, and they proceeded to demolish each other with Spartan-like heroism. Molly led off with a vicious right hander and smote Lizzie in the left optic, almost obscuring her vision. This caused Lizzie's blood to rise ten degrees in the thermometer and she led off with a vicious left-hander on Molly's larder almost knocking

the breath of life out of her. Hostilities then ceased for a time, and when they had gotten their breaths, again they proceeded with Sullivan-like viciousness to the combat. Lizzie being shorter and more vicious than her tall antagonist, led off with a wicked left-hander and caromed on Molly's lower ribs, brasing them to the Queen's taste, causing her bustle to stick out too much and bringing tears to her eyes. After recovering from this blow, and now being stung to fury, Molly led out with a paralyzing blow and erected a good sized shanty on the vacant lot between Lizzie's right eye and nose, and painting it a dark blue. At this point the referee declared a draw as Joe Martin and Marshal Snowden were hovering around, and the procession halted. The trouble arose over one of them wounding the young and tender affections of the other."

Blanche DeVille had a propensity for theft. She arrived in Silverton, stayed a very short time, then left. But, she stayed in the news while she was there. During the month of September 1884, alone, she robbed John Fernando, and was arrested. She was arrested again for stealing money from another soiled dove, Annie Williams. The grand jury indicted her for stealing $50 from prostitute Jessie Carroll. Blanche skipped town but was found and returned by her bondsman. To cap it off, she was thrown by a horse and broke her collar bone. All in the month of September.

The *Silverton Standard* reported another fight in its June 19, 1886, issue:

"Oregon Short Line is the euphonious alias of a lady of easy virtue, who constitutes a portion of the broadgauge system of Blair Street. Her carrying capacity was severely tested Tuesday night, in fact she was overloaded with wormy prunes and sour beer. 'Irish' Nell, 'Dutch' Lena and Minnie, 'the baby Jumbo' ... were on the warpath, spoiling for a fight ... and made it quite interesting for her (Short Line) for a few minutes. The scene of the accident was at the Alhambra on Blair Street. The expense to the belligerents was several black eyes, torn and disarranged costumes and $5 and trimmings assessed by his Honor, Police Justice Boyle."

Jealousy and drunkenness were often the cause of trouble. On December 8, 1900, the *Silverton Standard* reported:

"At 2 o'clock Wednesday afternoon, George Lynch was arraigned before the bar of justice, charged with having inflicted several smashes on the head of Miss Sidney Davis, of Blair Street, and also having smashed a mirror belonging to that lady to smithereens. From the testimony it appears that Mr. Lynch was drunk on the occasion, therefore, His Honor placed the penalty in moderation -- $10 and costs, which included the price of the looking glass -- total $36.85."

These are just isolated examples of Blair Street violence. There was much more. It is important to understand that with so many saloons, brothels, dance halls, and gambling dens, things were going to happen. Because of its reputation for "fun," people flocked to Blair Street from near and far, anxious for the action of the prostitutes and gaming tables. David Frakes Day, of Ouray's "Solid Muldoon", stated:

"Over in Silverton last week the society gentlemen attended a grand ball, and after they

36

had escorted their ladies home, cut loose and rounded up 'the scarlet daughters of prosperity,' repaired to the same hall and made Rome howl until daylight."

Among the girls on Blair Street, there existed a social stratum. Madames of the larger bordellos were held in high esteem. So were those most attractive girls (and there were some) who catered to a large following. On the low end were the prostitutes who worked in the cribs. As early as 1879 there were town ordinances to regulate gambling and prostitution. Neither were prohibited. Violators of either were guilty of a misdemeanor and, if convicted, received a modest fine. For the most part, city administrators did not want to clean up Blair Street. It provided the city with one of its primary sources of revenue. To keep face with the proper ladies of the community, arrests were made on occasion and fines imposed. The city fathers did make a concerted attempt to enforce certain ordinances in 1897. Gambling was actually shut down for about a week. After that, activity resumed as usual. The brothels and gambling halls hardly missed a heart beat -- they just kept running wide open.

A popular bordello was Jack Gilheany's "Laundry." According to one source, "If you went in with any money, you came out clean." The Laundry occupied the building that once housed Jane Bowen's Dance Hall and bordello. Good-hearted Gilheany is known to have returned part of some gamblers' losses to their wives, so their families could eat.

Jane Bowen didn't stay out of business long. After she sold her dance hall in March 1892, she purchased a lot in August of the same year and constructed the Palace Hall (later to become the National Hall). Three years later she added a large addition which was used entirely as a bordello. Eventually, these rooms would become Silverton's last house of prostitution, when they were occupied by "Jew" Fanny until about 1952.

There were many old-fashioned western brawls on Blair Street. The Louisa Dance Hall, which was owned by Louisa Crawford Matties, was the scene of one such fracas. It was reported by the *Silverton Standard*, on January 6, 1898, as follows:

"Jealousy, through unrequited love, worked up to a fever heat, by copious libations of bad whiskey, was the cause of the row that occurred, Thursday night at the dance hall formerly occupied by Louisa. Both thumping and pistol shots were indulged in; the piano player of the concern, at a very early stage of the game, having discharged his little 'pop' three times in rapid succession at the frontispiece of a gentleman from Mexico, who however, didn't get hit worth a cent, and, along with three companions also from Mexico mounted the marksman and hammered the life nearly out of him. The night watch, who was walking past the dance hall at the time of the fracas, heard a cry for help and upon entering the bar room, found the musician on the floor with the tropical gentlemen on top of him, beating the devil's tattoo on his head and ribs, while the frail, fair ones of the house stood around in an attitude of prayer. All the participants of the row were pulled, and yesterday were brought before Justice of the Peace Watson. From the testimony of the witnesses, it appears that a woman, who of late has been before the dread tribunal of justice quite frequently, and also, a Mexican woman, were the modern Delilahs, who brought their Sampsons to grief by capping up the row. Nearly all the witnesses were women of the avenue, only two or three having testified. The judge was very lenient and with the milk of human kindness oozing from his Websterian brow, he imposed fines on the discordant ones, of from five to ten dollars and costs, each."

As tensions increased prior to World War I, it was evident that the United States needed to increase metal production. A new mining boom was on. Business on Blair Street was bigger than ever.

The Bon Ton, Monte Carlo, Diamond Belle (Diamond Dance Hall), and the Tremount were some of the other large houses on Blair Street. Some of the smaller establishments were the Mikado, Tree Top, Arcade, "Fatty" Collins House, and the Green House. Many of the prostitutes after the turn of the century were as colorful as the earlier ones -- and they had colorful names as well. There was "Diamond Tooth" Leona, "Nigger" Lola, "Sheeny" Pearl, "Tar Baby" Brown, and the aforementioned "Jew" Fanny.

Silverton continued to serve bootleg whiskey during the period of Prohibition, without any pressure from local law enforcement officials. Everybody pitched in to move the whiskey to safe hiding whenever word was received that Federal Revenue agents were nearby. On those occasions when people were caught, they had their furniture and fixtures confiscated. Such action usually netted the government very little. The furniture and fixtures would be sold at public auction. Citizens would bid one cent on the dollar and would hold their bid without raising. An auction might net the government less than $10. Whoever had their furniture and fixtures confiscated would then pay the citizens one cent on the dollar to reclaim their items.

And so it was -- Blair Street -- a colorful page in Silverton history.

Up it came!

COLORADO'S ONLY SUBMARINE

The famous Civil War naval battle between the Monitor and Merrimac proved the effectiveness of ironclad ships and opened a new era in shipbuilding. The Merrimac had been sunk by the Federals when they abandoned the naval yard at Norfolk. Confederates raised the vessel, refurbished her, and covered her with iron plate. Ten heavy guns were mounted above her coat of armor. The ironclad Monitor was smaller, and housed a revolving iron turret which contained two guns. On March 9, 1862, in the harbor at Hampton Roads, Virginia, the two armored vessels battled for three hours, during which time neither did much damage to the other. The battle set the stage for ships of the future.

During the next fifty years, designers created all kinds of armored-steel ships. Battleships, cruisers, destroyers, torpedo boats, and submarines evolved from the planning stages to reality. One designer, R.T. Owens, lived in a most unlikely place for a ship designer -- Central City, Colorado. Submarines were not the invention of Owens -- a few had already been built. Owens believed that he had a better idea, and that he could design and build a submarine so efficient and sea worthy that the United States Navy would surely purchase his design. In 1898, Owens recruited the services of two carpenters, swore them to secrecy, and construction began. The ship was built inside the old Eclipse Livery Stable, which was rented for that purpose. The submarine was approximately eighteen feet long, and was constructed of hand-hewn lumber and stitched with square nails. The lumber was then covered with sheet metal. Rumors circulated that Owens was building a boat at the old stable, but nobody thought much about it. The townspeople never saw the boat -- they just heard the stories. After a while they didn't think much about it.

Missouri Lake is located about two and one half miles above Central City. Each year after the lake freezes over, residents flock there to ice skate. The lake had been exceptionally low during the fall of 1943 and subsequently froze that winter at a lower elevation than usual. Skaters could see a long, dark "cigar shaped" object beneath the ice. A section of ice was removed, and there it was -- a submarine lying on its side in about twelve feet of water.

There was much fanfare on January 26, 1944 for the raising of the sub. A crowd gathered to watch as a crane hoisted the submarine from the bottom of the lake. Never had there been a stranger sight in Gilpin County.

R.T. Owens had tested his submarine nearly a half-century earlier. The design would never have been of interest to the United States Navy, for the submarine wouldn't float.

Liz turned all eyes!

THE REFORMATION OF COCKEYED LIZ

Buena Vista was established in October 1879 and became an important supply and shipping center for the mining industry. It was also a smelter town. With a silver boom to the north at Leadville and a gold boom to the west at Saint Elmo, the streets of Buena Vista were full with clattering wagons loaded with ore, stagecoaches, carriages, and covered wagons. Soon the railroads came, and trains could arrive or depart in most any direction. The community was bustling with activity.

Buena Vista was a wild place in its early days. It is said that there were 68 places where a man could get a drink. Plentiful also were the brothels which catered to the desires of the predominantly male population. There were so many gamblers and prostitutes using assumed names that the post office had to establish a separate mail box for aliases. Early Buena Vista was virtually lawless. It was just the kind of town that Elizabeth Spurgeon was looking for.

Lizzie Spurgeon was a prostitute. On the day in 1886 when she stepped off the train, she created quite a commotion. Her lace trimmed, and brightly colored parasol matched her bright and fancy gown. Her hat was plumed high with feathers. Her full sleeves and frilly balayeuses swished as she walked. And, she walked with confidence, cutting her pale blue eyes at every man she could. There was no doubt in anyone's mind why Lizzie Spurgeon was in town.

She arrived from Pueblo, but how long she may have been there is uncertain. Her parents were among the earliest immigrants to the Kansas Territory -- and Lizzie was born in Kansas. Her background is a mystery. It was obvious, however, from her fancy attire that she had peddled her wares elsewhere before arriving at Buena Vista.

On the north side of Main Street, Lizzie purchased a choice lot. There she built a modest one-story brick house, and dubbed it the Palace Manor. Upon its completion, Lizzie's "girls" moved in and set up shop. The Palace, as it was commonly called, became the most notorious brothel in Buena Vista.

Lizzie was a highly desired prostitute -- even after her eye was knocked out of whack. Her business was an overnight success, much to the chagrin of another madam, Belle Brown. Belle had lost business and was jealous. One night she tanked up a group of rowdies, then sent the drunks over to the Palace to "tear up the joint." During the melee that followed, Lizzie was struck in the left eye and blinded. She lost control of the muscles in that eye as well. From that time henceforth, Lizzie was known as "Cockeyed Liz."

All the girls had their own favorites, and Lizzie was no

exception. Alphonse "Foozy" Enderlin was Buena Vista's only plumber. He was a frequent customer of the Palace and always "visited" Lizzie. He grew very fond of her. Likewise, she was always glad to see Foozy and looked forward to his visits. One day, out of the clear blue sky, Foozy popped the question, "Will you marry me?" Well, Lizzie was now 40 years old -- and she had been operating the Palace for over eleven years. She often tired from the strange hours. Lizzie said, "Yes." In order to make the occasion as romantic as possible, Foozy and Lizzie rented a carriage and "eloped" to Fairplay. They tied the knot on October 4, 1897.

Lizzie's girls moved out -- and Foozy moved in. He added an addition to the house which included two rental apartments. They rented out two of the girls' quarters also. Fancy that -- Buena Vista's hottest parlor house had become a "Bed and Breakfast." Stranger yet -- the popular prostitute and madam had become a respectable citizen. The fancy dresses and painted lips were gone -- replaced by conservative and demure attire. To make such a transformation within the same environment was quite an accomplishment.

For months, even years, men knocked on the door looking for Cockeyed Liz, or Pancake Fan, or one of the other girls. But, that never seemed to bother anybody. The callers were usually invited in for a drink and then sent on their way.

Lizzie died in 1929 at the age of seventy-two. Foozy passed away five years later. The two are buried beneath a single tombstone at the Mt. Olivet Cemetery in Buena Vista.

Samuel Adams

VOYAGE BEYOND THE BLUE

From its origins a few miles to the south, the Blue River flows northerly through the town of Breckenridge until it eventually dumps into the Colorado River near the present site of Kremmling. At one time, the river dropped rather uninterrupted for neither the Green Mountain or Dillon reservoirs existed. During the early exploration of the old West, there was speculation that a navigable water route could be found to the Pacific Ocean. Captain Samuel Adams had no idea how far it was to the Pacific Ocean nor how long it would take to get there, but he imagined that he could float down the Blue River into the Colorado River and on to points west, and he convinced quite a few people that it was possible.

With the financial backing of several Breckenridge residents, four boats were constructed of green lumber. Captain Sam recruited ten "sailors" to accompany him on his voyage. Amid much fanfare the expedition began in July 1869. Some Breckenridge ladies made a banner that read, "Western Colorado to California, Greetings." Equipped with a log for keeping records, some scientific instruments, firearms, and an ample supply of food, the crew set sail with two boats from a point north of Breckenridge. The other two boats were launched the second day, further downstream at a point now occupied by the Dillon Reservoir. There was a second celebration at which Judge Silverthorn made a speech.

It wasn't long before the hearty crew realized what was in store for them. They quickly encountered some rapids which capsized three of the four boats and left sailors hanging on rocks in the middle of the river. Captain Sam's papers and scientific instruments disappeared in the white waters of the Blue River. The expedition came to a temporary halt. While one of the sailors returned to Breckenridge for more instruments, the others repaired the boats. The first sign of dissension set in, and one crew member was sent packing with $30 in his pocket. Eventually the group was on its way again. A few miles further downstream, one of the boats crashed into a rock and was destroyed. The second set of instruments was lost. As dissension increased, four more crew members headed home.

Finally the explorers reached the confluence of the Blue and Colorado rivers on the 12th day of their expedition. As the Colorado roared through Gore Canyon, it became a maze of rapids, rocks, and waterfalls. The boat carrying most of the supplies went out of control and submerged. Most of the food was lost. Eventually the last boat was dashed upon the rocks and broke into pieces. More dissenters headed home.

A raft was constructed -- then another. The river consumed them in the same manner that it did the boats.

Almost a month had passed since the group had departed from Breckenridge. Most of the time was spent on shore, however, repairing boats, building rafts, waiting for new supplies, and simply drying out. With only two members of his original crew of ten remaining and his spirits thoroughly dashed by the torrents of the river, Sam Adam's expedition turned into an overland trek back to Breckenridge. The once unabashed and dauntless mariner returned to the snickers of the community. The tarnished and embarrassed Captain Sam was proclaimed to be, "a preposterous, 12-gauge, hundred-proof, kiln-dried, officially notarized fool."

Clara Brown

CLARA BROWN, PIONEER

Clara Brown was a black pioneer who truly left her mark on Colorado history. Clara was born in Virginia, and shipped to Kentucky at age three. Her parents were slaves. For much of her early life, Clara was owned by George Brown of Russellville, Kentucky. It was common for slaves to assume the last name of their masters -- such as Clara did.

Clara married another slave, and before he died she gave birth to four children -- Richard, Margaret, and the twins Eliza Jane and Paulina Ann. Paulina Ann died at a young age, and Margaret died in her teens. Richard and Eliza Jane were sold to different owners, and Clara feared that she would never see them again.

When George Brown died in 1856, his daughters decided to help Clara buy her freedom. Clara helped by contributing the $100 she had saved.

Clara went to St. Louis where she worked for nearly three years, saving every penny she could. In 1859 she joined a wagon train bound for Auraria, Colorado, and earned her passage by cooking. From there she gained passage on to Central City.

Upon her arrival at "the richest square mile on earth," Clara rented a two-room cabin and started a laundry. According to Clara, as soon as she had a sign painted saying "Laundry," she had customers. "Aunt" Clara, as she became known to the miners, had a thriving business and was able to save much money. Before long, she owned several houses in Central City and property elsewhere. She also became a part owner in some mining claims by grubstaking a few black miners who needed a start.

For years, Clara had missed her children and was now financially able to return to Kentucky to look for them. The Civil War was over, so she made the trip. She was unable to find either Richard or Eliza Jane, but her innate kindness was about to make an indelible imprint on mankind.

Following the war, many former slaves found life very difficult. Slave owners who had previously provided for their slaves, suddenly couldn't afford a payroll. Many slaves were simply turned out to fend for themselves. Also, the slave states were in a shambles and there simply weren't many available jobs. Clara gathered many former slaves together, paid their passage, and led them to Colorado. Her achievement -- especially for a woman nearing seventy years of age -- was remarkable, and touched the hearts of everyone.

Life began to get rough for Clara. She was cheated out of $4,000, spent most of the other money she had, and was becoming too elderly to operate her laundry. Before long she became ill and moved to Denver.

In 1881, Clara Brown was inducted into membership in the Society of Colorado Pioneers, becoming the first woman and the first black to be so selected.

The following year, Clara received word that her long-lost daughter Eliza Jane was living and working in Council Bluffs, Iowa. Friends donated money to pay Clara's fare, and she departed to find her daughter. Eliza Jane was found -- as was a granddaughter, Cindy, whom Clara never knew existed. Cindy accompanied Clara back to Denver, where she worked and took care of her ailing grandmother. Clara died at age 85.

Clara Brown is eulogized on a stained glass window in the Colorado State Capitol at Denver. The caption beneath her picture reads, "An ex-slave, who grubstaked miners and later led wagon trains of blacks from Kentucky to Colorado."

The George S. Lee Mansion

COLORADO'S OTHER CAPITOL CITY

In Hinsdale County, approximately ten miles west of Lake City, lies the site of Capitol City. Several good silver strikes in 1877 brought throngs of prospectors into the area. A townsite was platted, and tents were quickly replaced by substantial structures. George S. Lee built a sawmill to aid in the construction of Capitol City. Saloons, hotels, restaurants, and a general merchandise store sprang up. A post office was established in May of 1877.

Lee also constructed a smelter in 1879 along Henson Creek to process ore from the many mines nearby. The Ocean Wave Mine, which was located near the smelter, was one of the better producers in the vicinity. Other top mines were the Morning

Star, Capitol City, Yellow Medicine, and Polar Star. Much litigation over claim rights hampered the total production of the area, however.

It is said that George S. Lee had a dream that his town would become the capitol of Colorado (hence the name Capitol City) and that his home would become the governor's mansion. How much truth there is in the story, we don't know. We do know that he was overly optimistic with regard to the growth of the community. Lee and the town fathers planned a fine city with hotels, restaurants, stores, saloons, a schoolhouse, and more. Most of the dream never came to fruition. The Lee mansion was a different story.

George S. Lee built a large and elegant brick home. According to legend, the bricks were mailed to Capitol City, as post office rates were lower than those of freighting companies. The property sat in the shadows of the San Juan Mountains, on the bank of Henson Creek. Exterior lamps illuminated the grounds in the evening. In the house, which even contained a ballroom and orchestra pit, Mr. and Mrs. Lee lavishly entertained guests from near and far. In his book, *Colorado*, Frank Fossett called Lee's mansion, "the most elegantly furnished house in Southern Colorado." For purposes of fire protection, the kitchen was located behind the house in an outbuilding, where meals were prepared and then carried into the house where the dining room was located. As Capitol City had no plumbing, another of the buildings situated to the rear of the mansion was an outhouse.

After telephone service was established, a unique musical recital was held in 1881. Residents of Capitol City, Lake City, and communities as far as Silverton, who had telephones could pick up their receiver at a specified time and listen to the concert. In those days party lines could be connected. It is said that Mrs. Lee sang duets with a Mr. Bates in Lake City, while all who could listened.

The devaluation of silver in 1893 had a crippling effect on Capitol City. A few residents remained, but most moved on. The community experienced a brief revival when gold was discovered after the turn of the century, but it too was short-lived. During the good years, George S. Lee was very successful -- but his dreams for Capitol City never materialized.

He drew and fired

TIN CUP BLOOD

Tin Cup had the reputation of being one the wildest towns in Colorado. During the boom years, 26 saloons and gambling houses operated night and day. Parlor girls were quick to fleece a miner of his gold dust. Shootings and drunkenness were commonplace.

Owners of the saloons and gambling halls "controlled" Tin Cup. In 1880 a marshal was hired to give the town an appearance of being orderly. He was informed that the first person he arrested would be his last. The second marshal was also a pawn. He did little more than round up drunks, disarm them, and release them. By 1882 Tin Cup had become so lively that tough Harry Rivers was hired as marshal and instructed to maintain law and order. Rivers pushed his weight around, especially when he had too much to drink -- and such was his undoing.

Charley LaTourette moved from Leadville to Tin Cup in 1879 and opened a saloon called The White House. Like many saloon owners, LaTourette (whose given name was Koertenius LaTourette) was a fairly tough individual himself. He was a Civil War veteran who had served in the 115th, 133rd, and 154th regiments, and following the war he was said to have killed a man who threatened him.

One night Rivers had been drinking heavily. He saw that LaTourette was alone in The White House and decided to badger him. The marshal walked into the saloon and started hollering vile obscenities at LaTourette. Seeing that Rivers was drunk, the saloon owner ran him off. Business had been slow, so LaTourette decided to lock up and go home.

As he stepped from the boardwalk and started up Main Street toward his house, which was only a block away, Rivers began to follow him. The marshal pulled his gun and fired some "close" shots past LaTourette. As Charley LaTourette neared his home he realized that Emma, his wife, would open the front door when she heard the gate squeak -- as she always did -- and that she would be endangered. Before he reached the gate, LaTourette whirled, drew and fired. Marshal Harry Rivers dropped dead.

Charley LaTourette was exonerated by a kangaroo court in Tin Cup, and then again by Judge Sprigg Shackleford in Gunnison. This story has been told several times with one man or the other as villain. In actuality, Harry Rivers was an honest man who was a very good marshal when he was sober. Charley LaTourette was a businessman and family man who lived at home with his wife and adopted daughter. History records the happening as another gunfight in the old West.

She tossed down her most valued possessions

OH BE JOYFUL'S RESCUE

As the rowdy gold mining town of Tin Cup grew in size, it also grew in respectability. The "red light district" was once located on the south end of Grande Avenue during the boom days of the 1880s. It later moved into the alley between Washington Avenue and Main Street. The following events occurred in the late '80s.

The tarnished maidens usually slept during the daytime and plied their trade by night. Often the girls were "slaves" to their madams who usually had them "under contract." Such was the case with pretty and personable "Oh Be Joyful." Joyful's madam was stern and strict Deadwood Sal who allowed her no latitude.

61

Joyful fell in love with a young rancher from Gunnison and the couple wished to be wed. When they confronted Deadwood Sal with the idea of marriage, she would have none of it and reminded Joyful of her "contract." The couple pleaded but to no avail.

Joyful's suitor returned to Gunnison and discussed his dilemma with two friends. Together they devised a plan to rescue Oh Be Joyful from the clutches of Deadwood Sal. The task would not be easy, for Joyful's bedroom was upstairs above Deadwood Sal's. Careful preparation was made for the "escape." A moonless night was selected to carry out the plan. Joyful was notified so that she would be ready.

Everything unfolded as planned. The young suitor fetched the Justice of the Peace, and took him to a cabin two miles outside of town. Meanwhile, his two friends picked up a wagon which was waiting for them at the livery stable. They drove to the hose company and "borrowed" the town's fire ladder. They stopped the wagon around the corner from Deadwood Sal's place. Carefully and silently they propped the ladder at the open window where Joyful was waiting. She tossed down a bag which contained her most valued possessions, then quietly descended the ladder. The trio then rode swiftly out of town.

Shortly thereafter, they arrived at the cabin where the bridegroom and Justice of the Peace were anxiously waiting. The latter "tied the knot," then drove the wagon back to town. The bride and groom and their friends rode on to Gunnison. Everybody in town seemed to know what had happened, but Deadwood Sal would never discuss the matter with anyone.

Ridin' out a winter storm

BUCK ROGERS' LOST GOLD MINE

The lost fortune of Buck Rogers is perhaps Colorado's most authentic tale of buried treasure. In 1849 Buck Rogers and a group of prospectors left Illinois to join the gold rush in California. During their trek through present-day Colorado, the party found traces of gold near a peak they called Slate Mountain. While the others ventured on, six of the prospectors, including Buck Rogers, remained to work the area. Their efforts were rewarded when a rich vein was located. Gold was extracted which they estimated as worth up to $100,000. The ore was stored in a snowdrift until such time as it could be packed out.

When provisions ran low, Rogers set out with $500 in nuggets and dust for the nearest camp 150 miles away. The others remained in what may have been Colorado's first gold camp. After struggling through blizzards for many days, Rogers reached his destination. Winter storms and warm saloons delayed his return trip for several weeks, but finally he departed.

Upon returning to the location of the strike, Rogers was horrified at what he saw. An avalanche had carried snow and mud down the mountainside -- burying the camp, men, and the gold as well.

Following the incident, Rogers became a mental wreck -- and he tried to drown his conscience in whiskey. He spent his remaining years wandering from one saloon to another telling his woeful tale to all who would listen.

Forty years later amid new discoveries in the area, a settlement cropped up which was later to become Fulford. The camp was so named following the tragic death of Arthur H. Fulford -- which is another chapter in the Buck Rogers story. While operating a stage stop on the road from Eagle, Fulford had a visitor who claimed to have found human bones, tools, and a treasure of nuggets at a location which sounded much like the description of Slate Mountain. He had covered his discovery and was looking for a partner to help him pack out the gold. Fulford agreed to help. As they prepared for their trip, a strange twist occurred in the story -- the visitor was killed in a saloon brawl.

For months Fulford combed the gulches of the East Fork of Brush Creek, but to no avail. One day, while prospecting on nearby New York Mountain, fate dealt him the same cards that it did Buck Rogers' group years earlier. On New Year's Day 1892, an avalanche swept Fulford to his death.

During the ensuing years, many prospectors combed the area up East Brush Creek. As far as we know, no one has ever found the location of Buck Rogers' strike -- but, possibly one day someone will. Meanwhile, each time the story is told, the legend grows.

Otto Mears

THE LITTLE MAN WHO MOVED MOUNTAINS

Otto Mears was possibly the most important pioneer in the development of western Colorado. He was a road and railroad builder extraordinaire, who would take on any challenge. Impossible was not a word in his vocabulary. To accomplish his goals, the little man literally moved mountains -- or at least parts of them.

The native of Russia was orphaned at an early age, then shuffled from one relative to another -- to England and on to New York. At age fifteen, Mears was sent on to San Francisco to live with an uncle. When he arrived, there was no one to meet him for his uncle had gone to Australia. The lad was left to fend for himself. He worked odd jobs to pay for room and board. Following the Civil War, Otto Mears ventured to Colorado. He opened a store at Conejos in the San Luis Valley. Soon thereafter he built the first sawmill in the vicinity. He began growing wheat, then built a grist mill to grind his wheat into flour. In order to tap new markets, Mears built a road over Poncha Pass which opened up the Arkansas Valley and the gold boom area at California Gulch. He obtained the right to collect toll on his new road. This was just the beginning.

During the construction of a wagon road from Saguache to the San Juan mining country, an event happened that shaped the history of the area. Enos Hotchkiss, while under contract to Mears on the road project, found a little spare time to do some prospecting. In 1874 Hotchkiss made a rich gold strike above Lake San Cristobal at what was later to be named the Golden Fleece Mine. News spread, prospectors flocked to the area, and in 1875 the settlement of Lake City was incorporated.

As more and more rich discoveries were made further west, Otto Mears turned his attention to the San Juans. Pack trains could negotiate the mountain passes only during the summer, at which time it was necessary to haul supplies to all the settlements which became inaccessible during the winter months. In the fall of 1881 the Denver & Rio Grande railway began construction of the line from Durango to Silverton, with Otto Mears as its builder. When the Denver & Rio Grande arrived into Silverton on July 13, 1882, it marked the beginning of the town's greatest period of growth.

Transportation was a major problem for the mining settlements to the north, so Otto Mears went back to road building. He increased access to Ouray, and in doing so boosted its economy as well. He then turned his attention toward Red Mountain and the road which was the predecessor of the present Million Dollar Highway.

The site now generally called Red Mountain was once

known as Red Mountain Town and was the largest of the lucrative camps in the Red Mountain District. Guston and Ironton were substantial towns north of Red Mountain Pass. Additionally, Yankee Girl was a small camp adjacent to the Yankee Girl Mine near Guston. South of the summit were short-lived Red Mountain City and Sheridan Junction (Chattanooga).

Red Mountain (Red Mountain Town) became the largest and the most prosperous in the district. The camp which began in January 1883 was a boom town in two short months. Initially, the community was accessible from several directions -- and all were dangerous trails. The difficult access offered Otto Mears his greatest challenge to date. Finally the road was constructed, north from Silverton through Red Mountain and on to Ouray. An endless stream of wagons and pack trains traveled the new road.

The road was not enough, however, so Otto Mears built a railroad which connected with the Denver & Rio Grande at Silverton then snaked through the mountains to the north for twenty miles. The "Rainbow Route," as it was dubbed, arrived into Red Mountain in September 1888 amid much fan-fare. By November of the same year, the first train pulled into Ironton to another grand celebration. The rails of Otto Mears' Rainbow Route left Silverton and climbed across Red Mountain Pass at an elevation of 11,650 feet, then descended to Ironton. Upwards of 20,000 tons of ore were transported out of the Red Mountain District by train annually.

The Ophir Loop was one of Otto Mears' crowning achievements. A major construction project was necessary to enable the Rio Grande Southern to run from Telluride to Durango. A unique design was required to cross the gorge and change elevations. Mears met the challenge. Three tiers of tracks with loops crossing above and below each other and trestles sometimes one hundred feet high were the result of Mears' ingenuity. Depending upon how they reacted, passengers were either thrilled or chilled by the experience. According to legend, Otto Mears was so terrified during his first ride over the Ophir Loop that he wanted to get out and walk.

In 1896 Otto Mears completed his Silverton-Northern Railroad from Silverton to Animas Forks, which included a spur up Cunningham Gulch. The four-mile stretch between Eureka and Animas Forks was the hardest to build and most difficult to maintain. The canyon was narrow and the mountain slopes on each side were steep. Mears had hoped to minimize the constant hazard of slides by building snow-sheds throughout the route. To test the feasibility, he built one shed 500 feet long which was constructed of heavy timber, and thought to be impregnable. The snow-shed was wiped out by the first slide, and the others were never constructed. This was one of the few cases where the mountain had the upper hand.

Otto Mears was a true pioneer in Colorado and western history. He was called "The Pathfinder" by many, and the name fit him well. Mears had fought in the Civil War, served Kit Carson, helped negotiate treaties with the Ute Indians, and even served on the Board of Capitol Commissioners to construct the Colorado State Capitol. The orphan boy, who had supported himself by working odd jobs, had become a railroad magnate. Otto Mears died at the age of 91.

Leadville Ice Palace

THE GREAT ICE PALACE

It began in California Gulch in 1860 when Abe Lee discovered gold. Thousands flocked into the area to prospect the hills. When word spread in 1879 that the black sand throughout the region contained fifteen ounces of silver per ton, a second boom was on -- but this time it was silver. Nearly overnight, the city of Leadville developed into an extraordinary mining town with an air of elegance and sophistication. Many fortunes were made in Leadville -- many were also lost.

In 1893 President Cleveland repealed the Sherman Silver Purchase Act whereby the government would no longer purchase silver to back its currency. The foreign market for silver collapsed as well. Leadville was dealt a crippling blow, but it wasn't about to die.

The economy of Leadville rebounded magnificently. In 1895, silver production exceeded every year of Leadville's short history with the exception of the boom year of 1880. The total production of area mines was also the greatest since 1889. Once more, money was flowing. Seeking to bring tourists and new money into the community, several businessmen decided to create a new and different attraction -- an ice palace. Actually, the idea was not created by Leadville. Montreal and St. Paul had built similar structures. Leadville had talked about doing the same thing for some time, when suddenly the time seemed right.

Much time went into planning and design. Leadville wanted to build the finest such structure ever constructed. Finally the design was complete.

Huge blocks of ice were cut from the area's ponds and lakes. Some ice even arrived by rail. As many as 250 men were hired to cut the ice and build the palace which covered three acres of the five acre site. The structure looked much like a medieval castle -- a castle constructed with 5,000 tons of ice. Around the parameter were towers ranging from 60 to 90 feet in height. Within the confines of the five-foot thick walls, was a skating rink which was 80 feet wide by 190 feet long, a grand ballroom, and a large dining room.

The palace officially opened on January 3, 1896, amid much fanfare. City politicians, civic clubs, two thousand members of the Miners' Union, the Dodge City Cowboy Band, and others participated in a huge parade to commemorate the occasion. It was necessary for each of the three railroads serving Leadville to add extra passenger cars to scheduled trains in order to accommodate the throngs of tourists flocking to see the unique structure.

Visitors saw skating exhibitions, or could skate themselves. There was dancing and fine dining. Contests were held, and awards given for ice sculpting, skating, dancing, rock drilling, and for costumes.

It was fun while it lasted -- but it didn't last long. The winter of 1896 was unusually mild, and the ice began to melt prematurely. The uniqueness of the attraction began to wear off both to tourists and locals alike. The residents of Leadville grew tired of all the parties and festivities. The structure was also a financial failure. On March 28, 1896, the Ice Palace closed permanently.

John D. Morrissey

NO READIN', WRITIN', OR 'RITHMETIC

John D. Morrissey became rich and famous. His wealth was a result of the Leadville boom. His fame, however, was attributed to his illiteracy. Morrissey couldn't read or write, and his knowledge of mathematics was terrible.

According to one story Morrissey carried a bottle of whiskey to the portal of one of his mines. He hollered into the shaft, "How many of you are down there?" Their reply was, "Three." Morrissey yelled back, "Well, half of you come up and have a drink."

On one occasion, Morrissey was approached by one of

Leadville's churches and asked if he would donate the money for a new church chandelier. He said that he would, but expressed a concern as to its use, saying "I'll be damned if I know who would play on the thing."

John Morrissey couldn't sign his name. Being a businessman, his signature was often required on papers or documents. He had a number of excuses to avoid signing his name, such as, "My fist is frozen and I can't hold a pen." He once showed up at a hotel with a handkerchief wrapped around his hand, and told the hotel clerk, "Just write my name for me, young fellow. I just slammed the buggy door on my hand and hurt it."

He hated to admit that he couldn't write, and in the same manner he hated to admit that he couldn't tell time. Morrissey carried a fancy gold pocket watch studded with diamonds. When asked for the correct time, he would pull out his watch and say, "See for yourself, then you'll know I'm not lying to you." If he wanted to know the time himself, he would approach somebody and say, "I've made a bet with myself on the time of day." He would then pull out his watch and hand it over to the person while he continued his discourse. "I bet with myself that it's 7:35. If I'm right, we'll go into a bar and have whatever you would like to drink or smoke." Morrissey would never guess correctly, so his bet was always safe -- but he would find out the correct time.

On one occasion, while a resort hotel was being developed at nearby Twin Lakes, the owners agreed to purchase some gondolas for the use of their guests. They asked Morrissey how many he thought they should buy. His response was, "Just get two and let them breed."

Silverheels, the pride of Buckskin Joe

SILVERHEELS

The *Rocky Mountain News* once described Buckskin Joe as South Park's "liveliest little burg." Half the residents are said to have made their living from the several saloons, gambling halls, and billiard parlors. From the rowdy mining camp which sprang to life following a placer strike in 1860, grew the legend of Silverheels.

No one seems to know her real name, or where she came from. She was a dance hall girl named Silverheels -- so named because of the silver heels on her dancing shoes. All the men in camp clamored for a chance to dance with her, for she was a girl of much charm and extraordinary beauty.

During the cold winter of 1861, an epidemic of smallpox

swept through the mining community. Mines, stores, and saloons shut down. Most of the miners became desperately ill, and many died. There was a steady trek to the little cemetery on the hill in order to bury the dead. Silverheel's boyfriend died in her arms. Requests for nurses went unheeded, for women were not willing to risk their lives or their looks by subjecting themselves to the highly contagious disease which left its victims pockmarked for life.

Throughout the ordeal, Silverheels went from cabin to cabin caring for the sick and comforting the dying. She scrubbed, and cooked, and nursed. Finally she too was stricken by the illness.

When the epidemic subsided, miners collected $5,000 in cash as a gift for Silverheels to show their gratitude for what she had done. The men carried the reward to her cabin only to find that she had disappeared.

Some time later a woman dressed in black, and heavily veiled, was seen in the cemetery -- weeping. When approached she quickly departed. Had Silverheels come back to mourn her friends? The miners certainly thought so. She had sacrificed her beauty and thereafter shunned her former admirers. For her valor a majestic peak, Mt. Silverheels, was named in her honor. The silvery snow on the summit somehow reminds one of the dancing shoes once worn by the courageous heroine of Buckskin Joe.

*   *   *   *   *   *   *

[Note: There may be some truth in this story -- then again, it may be part of Colorado mythology. Nothing is written to authenticate the story of Silverheels. That's not to say, however, that it couldn't have happened. There was no newspaper in South Park in 1861. Neither Father Dyer nor anyone else ever recorded an epidemic at Buckskin Joe during that year. Similarly, there is nothing in the Buckskin Joe cemetery which would substantiate the story. But then again there probably wouldn't be. The graves would have been among the earliest in Colorado mining history. Buckskin Joe had nobody to chisel or cast headstones in 1861. Graves at that time took on several forms. Often the perimeter of the burial plot was lined with rocks. Sometimes a pile of rocks would be placed at the head of the grave site. In a few cases the entire site would be covered by rocks. Inscribed wooden markers probably would have weathered away. It is important to remember, also, that during an epidemic graves were usually hastily prepared. Some historians believe that the story is strictly myth -- and they may be right. Then again, it may have happened. At any rate, the legend has been passed down through the years and remains a part of the legacy of mining camp stories.]

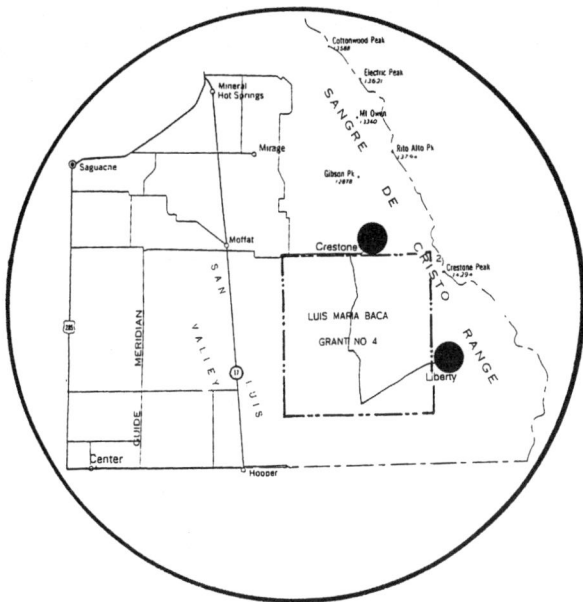

Luis Maria Baca Grant No. 4

THE BACA GRANT: ITS EFFECT ON AREA MINING SETTLEMENTS

In 1822 King Ferdinand the Seventh of Spain bestowed upon one of his subjects the title of Don Luis Maria Cabeza de Vaca and granted him several hundred thousand acres of land in the west which included a 100,000 acre tract in Saguache County. The grant is known as the Luis Maria Baca Grant No. 4. The northeastern portion of the tract cuts into the Sangre de Cristo Range where deposits of gold, silver, lead, copper, and iron were found.

Prospectors began picking at the rocks in these mountains about 1879 and found some gold. A mild flurry of activity occurred, and several small mining camps cropped up. Those established within the boundary of the grant were Duncan, Cottonwood, Lucky, Spanish, Teton, and Julia City. Just beyond the northern border of the Luis Maria Baca Grant, and nestled below the Crestone Needle, lies the townsite of Crestone. Its post office was established in 1880. Many Crestone residents lived within the perimeter of the grant.

The flurry of activity dwindled until free-milling gold was found in 1890, and a greater boom developed. It was during this time that Crestone became a substantial settlement. During the 90s the old Cleveland Mine was reopened, and the nearby camp of Wilcox sprang up north of town. Lesser camps were scattered through the foothills for miles.

Duncan and Cottonwood were the largest of the settlements located within the boundary of the grant. Each had about one thousand residents. Outside the boundary, the population of Crestone had reached nearly two thousand by 1898, and activity was at its peak. A railroad was constructed from Moffat. There were five general stores, a hotel, and several specialty shops and saloons. Prime commercial lots sold for up to $600. Many Crestone residents relied on the mining properties within the grant for their income -- and many of the best properties were within the boundary.

When the value of land and minerals became evident, grant owners began proceedings to close the settlements and evict the miners. In 1898 the Supreme Court upheld the provisions of the Luis Maria Baca Grant giving the owners excessive powers to create leases based on royalties. Meanwhile an eastern company purchased the mineral rights on the grant and a half interest in the townsite of Crestone. After some violence, the U.S. Circuit Court issued a summons to evict the remaining "squatters," allowing only those who were employees of the San Luis Valley Land and Mining Company to remain. The camps were actually closed in 1900 and miners were forced to move on. Many of those who moved from the Baca Grant property re-established residence outside the boundary at either Crestone or Liberty. Others moved on in disgust.

Crestone settlers watched the mines they had worked so hard to build become the property of others. Some persevered however. New mining activity which occurred in 1901 bolstered the hopes of some that the sagging economy might be sustained, but the optimism was short-lived.

William Gilpin (later to become Governor of Colorado) was among the early prospectors in the area. He discovered some gold while traveling with John Fremont, the famed pathfinder. Gilpin helped establish the original camp at Duncan which temporarily became deserted prior to the 1890 boom.

The community of Duncan was located just inside the eastern boundary. It had a school with 40 students, a few stores, a bunkhouse, and a newspaper -- *The Golden Eagle.* When eviction occurred, miners moved their buildings and all a short distance outside the grant and named the new community Short Creek, then Liberty -- so named because they were "free" of the grant and its problems. A few miners remained on the grant to work for the San Luis Valley Land and Mining Company which had taken over the mines inside the boundary.

Once Liberty was established, more money was pumped into the vicinity. The Blanca Mutual Mining and Milling Company built a five-stamp mill in 1902. Mining dwindled during the ensuing years, however, and by 1909 the Liberty school had but three students -- all from the same family. The schoolhouse which had once been in Duncan, then moved to Liberty, was moved again -- this time to Crestone, in 1910. Many cabins were moved also, as most of the mining was discontinued. A hermit maintained residence at the camp long after everyone else had left. He was "touched," it is said, and collected animal bones which he displayed for the occasional passer-by.

Crestone settled back to become the quiet community that it is today. Many of the mines within the grant proper produced well into the twentieth century. Cattle raising is now the principal business on the huge ranch known as Luis Maria Baca Grant No. 4.

John C. Breckinridge

HOW BRECKENRIDGE GOT ITS NAME

Although there were a number of exploratory expeditions through the valley along Blue River during the 1840s and 1850s, there was no permanent settlement until 1859. In August of that year, a group of southerners from Georgia and Alabama led by ex-General George E. Spencer descended into the area and began to pan the stream.

History records that Ruben J. Spalding worked his first pan for gold that was valued at thirteen cents. His second pan was worth twice that. Another prospector in the group, William H. Iliff, washed out $7,000 worth of gold from a 40 square foot area across the stream. Convinced that they had just touched the surface, the group constructed a log fort for protection from the Indians, and the settlement that would become Breckenridge was started.

Spencer was instrumental in naming the new town after a fellow southerner, John C. Breckinridge, the current Vice-President of the United States during the administration of James Buchanan. This helped hasten the establishment of a post office which occurred January 18, 1860.

During the ensuing year Buchanan softened in his sentiments toward the southern cause for slavery and lost favor with the north. In the Presidential Election of 1860 the new Republican Party candidate, Abraham Lincoln, won election over three other candidates -- Democrat Stephen A. Douglas, Southern Democrat John C. Breckinridge, and John Bell of the Constitutional Union Party. Chagrin over the town's name had set in.

The southern sympathizers who founded the settlement were soon a small minority as tents and log cabins blossomed up and down Main Street. As the population swelled, eastern "Yankees", a large contingency in the community, subtly changed the town's name to avoid further embarrassment. The first "i" was replaced by an "e" and the name Breckenridge was born.

Bull fight at Gillett, 1895

SPORTS AND RECREATION IN "THE WORLD'S GREATEST GOLD CAMP"

Dubbed "the world's greatest gold camp" the Cripple Creek Mining District was the fifth largest gold producing district in the world. The gold production for the district has been estimated at a half-billion dollars. Cripple Creek, Victor, Goldfield, and many smaller communities comprised the district which created several millionaires. Seldom has there been a mining community that put more into sporting activities, recreational facilities, and general entertainment for its citizens.

Miners and their families worked hard during the week and looked forward to the weekends as a time to celebrate. The

Cripple Creek Mining District, like other districts, turned out en mass for holiday festivities. Fourth of July and Labor Day parades were long and joyous. Every time a circus came to town (and there were many) thousands again turned out for the colorful circus parade. Cultural life centered around the theaters and opera houses. Patrons usually paid between 15 cents and 35 cents to attend a stage attraction. Cripple Creek's Grand Opera House had many uses. The Grand would fill to capacity to watch such prizefighters as former heavyweight champions Jack Dempsey (who once worked at the Portland Mine) and Jack Johnson. The first indoor rodeo in history was also held at the Grand. Rodeos were quite popular in both Victor and Cripple Creek. Crowds of 5,000 people would pack Cripple Creek's Union Park for baseball games which, on a regular basis, attracted the largest audiences.

Millionaires Frank and Harry Woods, discoverers of the Gold Coin Mine, poured much money back into the area's recreation. Adjacent to the small town of Cameron, whose peak population barely exceeded 400, the Woods Investment Company constructed a wonderful recreational area -- Pinnacle Park. The thirty acre park was constructed at a cost of $32,000. There was a fine zoo, a dance pavilion, restaurants, a stadium which seated 1,000 people, and other amenities. The Labor Day celebration in 1900 was attended by 9,000 persons. Admission was 10 cents per person.

Pinnacle Park was architecturally very attractive. The dance pavilion and each of the buildings had hip-roofs. On square structures such as towers, the roofs were hip-pyramids. Buildings had exteriors of wood diagonally cut at 45 degrees. This look was carried throughout the park, on the pavilion's gables, on a bridge, even on some fences.

The Woods brothers also built the magnificent Gold Coin Club in Victor which housed a ballroom, gymnasium, bowling alleys, a billiard room, and other facilities.

Although it was a mining town and a railroad town, Gillett is most famous for its recreation. A half-mile racetrack, Sportsman's Park, on the north edge of town was the site of many horse races for several years. Many of the top horses of the day drew up to 3,000 race fans on a single afternoon. Gillett is best remembered, however, for its bull ring which was constructed in 1895 inside the oval at the racetrack.

Upon completion of the bull ring, J.H. Wolfe and his co-promoters staged a three-day "fiesta" August 24-26, 1895. The event was highly advertised. Matadors and bulls were imported from Mexico. Tickets sold for $5.00 each day. Whether or not the bulls were tired from their trip to Colorado is not known, but they refused to fight. One was tortured for twenty minutes before it was killed, and the show turned into a fiasco. On the up-side, the bulls were slaughtered and steaks were distributed to the poor. The promoters' expenses of $7,000 exceeded the total receipts of $2,600. One of the few bull fights ever staged in this country was a flop.

During the winter months, both towns had illuminated ice skating rinks.. The rink at Cripple Creek opened annually as part of the festivities of the Elks Club Winter Carnival.

There was always much to do in "the world's greatest gold camp."

Scotty found a new audience for his stories

BROKEN NOSE SCOTTY

Once a stagecoach driver, Broken Nose Scotty received his name after incurring injuries from a runaway stage near Weston Pass. Scotty was a storyteller and a dreamer. Like so many others in the Leadville area, he turned to prospecting, certain that instant wealth would be in his future. During the week he would diligently work his claim on Breece Hill. During the weekends he frequented Leadville's barrooms where he loved to tell stories of his harrowing experiences as a stage driver.

One Saturday night in 1879, Broken Nose Scotty became very drunk and disorderly. It wasn't long before the stiff arm of the law carried him to the jailhouse and locked him up. The

89

jail was crowded, and he immediately found a new audience for his stories.

The following morning Scotty had a visitor who wanted to buy his claim. They agreed upon a price of $30,000. Scotty was released from jail, and the two went straight to a lawyer's office to draw up the papers. The deal was consummated.

Scotty was ecstatic -- he had never seen so much money. He wanted everyone to share his happiness. Gleefully, he returned to the jailhouse, and "bailed out" all of his "friends." Together they all went to the haberdashery and were outfitted from head to toe with new clothes. The group proceeded on to the Tontine -- early Leadville's most fashionable restaurant. Champagne and the finest meals were ordered for everyone. They ate and drank, then drank some more -- and all wound up back in jail for disturbing the peace.

It is said that Broken Nose Scotty provided a trust to take care of his aging mother. Scotty spent the rest of his money and eventually died a pauper -- with the county paying his burial fees.

George Skinner found a fortune

LOST BROTHER - LOST GOLD

The thought of striking it rich fueled a million dreams. Some of those dreamers traveled to Colorado, certain that their vision would become reality. One of those was George Skinner, who left his home in Illinois and ventured in to the Wet Mountain Valley to prospect in the Sangre de Cristo range. He had asked his brother Bill to make the trip with him, but Bill decided to remain in Illinois.

Bill received one letter, several months after George had departed. He still tried to convince Bill to head for the Sangre de Cristos. The letter glowed with optimism. George was sure that he would soon find a fortune. Furthermore he gave Bill directions on how to find him should he decide to follow.

Months went by and a second letter never came. Then the months stretched into years, and still there were no letters. Bill feared the worst.

The silence gnawed at him until finally he decided to head west and find George. He packed light -- but was careful to include George's letter -- then departed. It was a long journey to the Wet Mountain Valley, but finally he arrived. The valley was long, and the mountain range vast. Bill knew it would be like looking for a needle in a haystack. He inquired of nearly every prospector he saw as to his brother's whereabouts. Nobody seemed to know. Weeks went by, then suddenly Bill had a lead. An old fellow told him, "I remember a guy named Skinner, but I haven't seen him for a couple of years. It seems like he was prospecting up on Horn's Peak." It was the first good news Bill had heard. He hired a guide with a burro, and the two of them set out for their destination. They searched and searched but to no avail.

One afternoon as a storm swept upon them, they stumbled on an abandoned log cabin and decided to seek refuge there until it blew over. The heavily-packed burro stood outside with his neck through a window in order to keep his head dry. The storm soon subsided and they set out again. Just a short piece up the trail, the usually sure-footed burro slid on some wet mud and tumbled down the mountainside to his doom. Knowing that the burro couldn't have survived, Bill and his guide carefully climbed down to retrieve as many of the supplies as they could carry.

When they reached their dearly departed burro at the bottom of the gulch, they spied two skeletons nearby. One was a human, the other a burro with his pack still strapped around his bones. They also must have slipped off the narrow, treacherous little trail above. Bill approached the skeletons, unstrapped and opened a leather pouch. He and his guide couldn't believe their eyes -- the pouch contained a fortune in gold dust! Bill spotted another leather pouch and opened it as well. Inside was a diary and some papers. Bill's heart fell to his stomach. Written inside the cover was, "George Skinner's Diary." His worst fears were realized -- there lay George. Inside the diary was an unfinished letter, dated two years earlier, to his brother Bill. George wrote that he had discovered rich gold -- bright enough to "blind a body." He added that there was plenty of it. He wanted Bill to know about it, and where it was, in case something should happen to him. George carefully described the gulch which lay below his mine. Bill's guide indicated that he knew exactly where it was. But the letter stopped there. There were no specific details on how to find the mine. How incredible, thought Bill as he buried the remains of his brother and the two burros, that George had met his maker two years ago and nobody had found him.

On the following day, snow began to fall, so Bill and his guide retreated from Horn's Peak. They agreed that they would return in the spring to find George's mine. They did return the following spring -- and the next spring as well -- but they never found the mine. Nor has anyone else. No gold of such richness has ever been found in the vicinity. Evidently the gold is still there waiting to be rediscovered.

Silverton had its share of gunfights

GUNFIGHTS ON GREENE STREET

The ink on the Brunot Treaty was barely dry when the townsite of Silverton was surveyed and platted in 1874. The treaty (with the Ute Indians) opened the area for white settlers, and they wasted no time establishing a community. The first structures were log, but as soon as a sawmill was in place construction was all wood frame. The law in early Silverton had its ups and downs. Occasionally the citizens took matters into their own hands. The first sheriff in the vicinity was also the mail carrier. The first lawbreaker was chained to the floor of a cabin, for a jail had not yet been built.

When Silverton was platted, the east-west streets were numbered, and those running north and south were given names.

Greene Street is the main street through Silverton's central business district. Originally it was lined with many saloons and dance halls. There was the Rose Bud, the Crystal Palace, the Olympic, the Diamond Saloon, the Arlington (where, for a while, the gambling was run by Wyatt Earp), Westminster Hall, Brown and Cort's (later to become the Tivoli), the Star of the West, Johnnie Goode's, and the Arion.

Like many towns in the old west, Silverton had a few gunfights. The first of consequence occurred in October 1878 after an argument and fistfight between Tom Milligan and Bill Connors. Connors wouldn't let the matter drop and told Milligan that he would shoot him the next time he saw him. Shortly thereafter as Milligan was walking down Greene Street he spotted Connors in front of the Silverton Hotel. Both men drew, and Milligan shot Connors through the stomach. Connors died three days later. Milligan was acquitted on the grounds of self defense.

Following the re-election of James Cart as town marshal, Silverton's newspaper, the *La Plata Miner*, made the following statement on April 12, 1879, " ... The re-election of Mr. Cart is a guarantee of order and respect for the law the coming summer." Ironically, "the coming summer" was a bloody one.

One night the following month, while walking his beat, handicapped night watchman Hiram Ward encountered the Dermody brothers, James and Pete, who had been boozing it up at the Westminster Hall. They exchanged words before the brothers headed home. Like most Irishmen, the Dermodys loved their whiskey, and the following night (May 27, 1879) they were at it again. This time at Goode's Saloon. Ward walked in, and once again the trio exchanged words. Ward told the brothers to go home and sleep it off. James Dermody told Ward to mind his own business. Ward pushed Dermody outside on to Greene Street and a fight began. Dermody bit Ward then wrestled him into the ditch. Getting the worst of the scuffle,

Ward drew his gun and shot James Dermody dead. The press called the shooting "uncalled for." Hiram Ward was found innocent. He was soon to be back in the news again.

There are several variations to the Harry Cleary story, and this is one of them. On August 23, 1879, Cleary and "Mexican Joe" became very rowdy while drinking at Brown and Cort's Saloon on Greene Street. James M. (Ten Die) Brown, one of the saloon's owners, escorted Cleary out the front door. Cleary turned and shot Brown. Brown was able to get off some shots, and one stray bullet hit night watchman Hiram Ward in the left shoulder. Ward, in turn, also shot Brown. More than likely it was one of Ward's bullets that penetrated Brown's heart, but Cleary was blamed for the killing, arrested and jailed. Late that night a mob dragged Cleary from the jail house and lynched him behind the blacksmith shop. It was later agreed by most that if Cleary's bullet had penetrated Brown's heart, Brown would never have been able to fire off the rounds which he did. Hiram Ward was never prosecuted for any wrong doing.

At 11 p.m. on August 24, 1881, La Plata County Sheriff, Luke Hunter, arrived in Silverton with warrants for the arrest of members of the Stockton-Eskridge gang. Burt Wilkinson, Dyson Eskridge, and the "Copper Colored Kid" (a black man) had been drinking at the Diamond Saloon. Sheriff Hunter rounded up Silverton's marshal, D.C. (Clate) Ogsbury. As the two men walked down Greene Street, Wilkinson and Eskridge opened fire killing Ogsbury instantly. The two escaped on foot while the "Copper Colored Kid," who apparently fired no shots, rounded up their horses. He was apprehended near the stable and carried to jail. Once again, a mob took the law into its own hands as they dragged the black lad from jail and lynched him behind the old county building.

Burt Wilkinson was turned in for a $2,500 reward by the gang leader Ike Stockton. Once again, the mob ruled. According to the *San Juan Herald*:

" ... a party of masked men suddenly appeared before the guards at the jail and overpowered both of them and the jailer, went into the jail and seizing Wilkinson, passed the noose about his neck and asked him if he had anything to say before his death. He replied, 'Nothing gentlemen, Adios!' He was perfectly composed to the very last, got up on a chair and assisted the vigilantes to hasten the hanging."

About a month later, Stockton was shot in Durango by Deputy Sheriff Jim Sullivan. Nobody would fetch a doctor, and he was left alone to bleed to death.

Silverton's city officials solved part of the problem the following year with the construction of a new "mob proof" jail. According to the *San Juan Herald*:

"The interior arrangement consists of two cells or cages placed in the center of the building. They are made of the best Bristol steel. ... The cells are guarded by four locks each and four on the door that leads from the main corridor to the small one inside the enclosure. The outside door is built of solid iron and is guarded by an immense 300-pound lock of the most approved patterns ..."

During the ensuing years, there were other shootouts in Silverton. Among the most memorable, however, were those *Gunfights on Greene Street* during the earlier years.

Thomas Walsh

THOMAS WALSH AND THE CAMP BIRD

Nineteen year old Thomas Walsh departed from his native Ireland in 1869, bound for the United States. Accompanied by his father and sister, the young carpenter set out to join his brother who was already living in the U.S.. Bridge building brought him to Colorado, and he was employed for awhile by the Colorado Central Railroad constructing its line into Black Hawk. He then moved north to Deadwood, South Dakota, where he operated a carpenter shop for just over one year. With money in his pocket, Walsh returned to Colorado and joined the throngs pouring into the boom town of Leadville, where he became a partner in the hotel business. The year was 1878. The following year he married Carrie Bell Reed, a school teacher. Walsh invested into some mining properties at Leadville before he and Carrie moved to Denver. Walsh and his bride were becoming wealthy. He established a real estate business and accumulated more property.

After a while, things began to turn sour for Thomas Walsh. He sold some properties, others were heavily mortgaged, and his debts had increased dramatically. A few of Walsh's investments failed, and the silver crash of 1893 crippled others. In the summer of 1896, Walsh and his family moved to Ouray. By this time his financial condition had worsened. To gain enough capital to keep a smelter he owned in Silverton operating, he had to sell some of his better leases. He had to find new mines which would ship ore to his smelter, as well. The fortunes of Thomas Walsh were about to change for the better, however.

Mine owners often shipped samples to smelters with the hope that the smelter might purchase their ore. Is it possible that samples from the Imogene Basin area had gold values which were not reported with those of silver, lead and other metals common to the basin? Walsh rapidly began to acquire claims in Imogene Basin. The devaluation of silver naturally devalued silver mines. He was able to purchase many for a "song." Others he acquired on tax title. Furthermore he took over some old abandoned claims, and staked new ones. Somehow Walsh knew there was rich gold ore in the basin -- ore that others had thought to be simply low-grade. He had struck it rich!

Thomas Walsh accumulated 129 mining claims which covered 1200 acres, then consolidated them under the name Camp Bird Mines. He virtually controlled the vein which extended from Imogene Basin to Ironton. Assay values ranged between $40 and $3,000 per ton. It wasn't long before his mining property produced over $1,000,000 per year and it eventually became the second largest producer in Colorado (only the Portland Mine near Cripple Creek was larger).

For his employees Walsh built posh boardinghouses. The facilities which accommodated 400 men had marble-topped lavatories, electric lights, steam heat, china plates, and even a piano. Meals were often served that rivaled the finest restaurants.

Walsh was already a multi-millionaire when he sold the Camp Bird properties, in May 1902, to an English syndicate for 3.5 million dollars in cash, a half-million in shares of stock, and royalties on future profits. To show his gratitude, the generous Thomas Walsh gave employees bonus checks of up to $5,000. Before his death in 1910, he had received 6 million dollars from the sale of the Camp Bird.

Thomas and Carrie Walsh had one daughter, the flamboyant Evalyn Walsh McLean who wrote a book entitled *Father Struck It Rich*. When Evalyn married Edward B. McLean, whose family owned the *Washington Post*, the newlyweds received $100,000 from each family as a wedding gift. Later Evalyn purchased the famous Hope Diamond which she dangled in front of Washington and Denver society.

To hell you ride!

TO HELL YOU RIDE

Whoever referred to Telluride with a play on words, "To hell you ride!", wasn't far wrong. According to historian Frank Hall, there were always "more than a sufficiency of saloons" in Telluride. Gambling dens such as Pacific Hall were quick to fleece a miner of his hard-earned wages -- so were the brothels. Parlor houses were important in most all predominantly male mining towns, and Telluride was no exception. Its "sporting" establishments ranged from the elegant Pick and Gad, a popular bordello, down to the simple cribs.

It all began when John Fallon discovered the Sheridan vein ten miles east of Telluride in August of 1875. The lode was tapped by other claims -- the Union, Mendota, and Smuggler.

The Smuggler was the result of a brilliant deduction by J.B. Ingram. Ingram thought that both the Sheridan and Union claims seemed too large. He discovered that both exceeded their legal allowance by several hundred feet. So, he staked the Smuggler on the area covered by the excess. Following mergers and purchases, the Smuggler-Union emerged as the area's biggest producer. By the turn of the century, the company had 35 miles of tunnels. By that time, the Liberty Bell and the Tomboy had also emerged as top producers as well. In later years, several properties were purchased by the Idarado Mining Company. With advanced milling methods, Idarado became the largest producer of all.

Along the San Miguel River, the small camp named Columbia cropped up in the late '70s. In 1881 its name was changed to Telluride. Although its location was rather isolated, Telluride's growth was steady through the 1880s. The community, and the mining industry on which its economy was reliant, received a real boost with the arrival of the railroad in 1890.

Many have referred to Telluride as "hell," but it had another side also. To occupy the leisure time of those so inclined, there were many civic clubs, fraternal organizations, dances, and concerts. Ethnic groups had their own meeting places such as Swedish Hall and Finn Hall. Much advance preparation was made each year for the huge Fourth of July celebration. Fireworks, a huge parade, and a grand ball highlighted the festivities. This other side, however, was greatly overshadowed, as Telluride was most noted for its lawlessness.

Once, while considering relocation, a Bostonian lady wrote to a Telluride official inquiring about the town's society. According to legend (and Sandra Dallas), the Telluride official's reply was as follows: "As for sowciety it is bang up. This is a mighty morrell town considerin that theres 69 saloons and two newspapers to a poppylation of 1,247. ... Only two men has been killed since Monday. ... Cheatin at gamblin is punished by linchin. ... Ladies is universally respected and I sell them beer at half price when they buy at my place ... preachin every Sunday that the preacher dont have ter stay ter home on account of the big rush at his bowlin alley. Dont hezzytate about comin here on account of sowciety. This a morrel town."

A man with many enemies was the town marshal, Jim Clark. He was a crack shot who carried two pistols and stashed rifles at strategic locations around town in case he needed one in a hurry. In return for favors from storekeepers, Clark would bully debtors into paying their bills. While walking his beat one night, a shot rang out from the darkness between two stores and killed him instantly. Nobody knew who fired the shot -- and, nobody really cared.

In broad daylight one afternoon in 1889, with the help of two sidekicks, Butch Cassidy robbed his first bank in Telluride. Cassidy and his pals rode out of town with a posse hot on their heels. Legend has it that they were pursued so closely that they didn't have time to switch to fresh horses hidden south of Telluride -- and, weeks later skeletons of the horses were found tied to a tree.

The biggest bank heist, however, occurred years later and was an inside job. Following the crash of 1929, many banks failed. When Charles Waggoner, president of the Bank of Telluride, couldn't cover the deposits of his Telluride friends, he felt as though he had to do something quickly. By using certain banking codes, he had large drafts deposited by top New York banks to the credit of his bank. He covered the deposits of his Telluride friends, and in an effort to hide the rest of the money he scattered it across the country in smaller deposits. The fraud totaled a half million dollars. Waggoner was arrested and imprisoned, but to the people of Telluride he was a hero.

Much of the violence which occurred in Telluride was a

result of the labor war. The Western Federation of Miners called a strike at the Smuggler-Union on May 2, 1901, to protest wages based on quantity of ore mined rather than the standard three dollar rate for eight hours which was common throughout most of the state. After six weeks of inactivity, mine owners hired non-union "scabs" at wages of three dollars per day, and reopened the mines. A confrontation occurred between 250 armed and irate union workers and the non-union men. After three men were killed and six more injured, the scabs were run out of town. The strike was settled and the union had won the first round. The mine owners won the second round, however, and they won it big. Miners at the Tomboy struck in September of 1903 when the new mill was opened with non-union workers. Faced with a new threat of impending violence, Governor James Peabody declared a state of martial law. The militia seized control. Union laborers and union sympathizers were loaded in rail cars and run out of town. Many were beaten first. A statement was issued by the mine owners: "...We do not recognize a union in Telluride. There is no strike in Telluride. There is nothing to settle."

Not all of the "hell" in Telluride resulted from fists, guns, and "painted women." Every winter there existed the threat of snowslides. A series of disastrous slides started in March of 1902. One hit the Liberty Bell sweeping away the aerial tramway and several men. A second slide buried a rescue party which was searching for bodies. The following day another drift forced a new group of rescuers to return to town. Meanwhile, a Cornish miner started the trek from ten miles east of Telluride to join the rescue effort. He was also buried by a snowslide. No bodies were uncovered for some time, and it was months before the Cornish miner was found. Telluride was devastated by the chain of events.

For many years, silver was the backbone of Telluride's economy. Following the silver crash in 1893, the mining industry turned its attention to gold. Today, the economy thrives on tourism -- and indeed its future is bright. Telluride is experiencing dramatic expansion as a year-round resort. The town itself, which is nestled on the floor of a gorgeous, spectacular box canyon, looks much as it did a century ago -- with Victorian homes laced with gingerbread and topped with tin roofs. The scenic hills above, however, are in the midst of exciting development. Telluride has become a playground for many movie stars and other celebrities, and some have built beautiful homes in the area. Also, new resorts are popping their heads above the treetops. The future looks very bright indeed.

Caverna del Oro

CAVERNA DEL ORO

Near Westcliffe, above the Wet Mountain Valley, high in the Sangre de Cristo Mountains is the Caverna del Oro. For years the cave has held much mystique. Caverna del Oro is Spanish for "Cavern of Gold," and through the years legends have been told about the existence of gold in the cave.

According to early Spanish legend, Indians used the gold as an offering to their gods. Later stories tell of conflicts between the Indians and the Spaniards over the gold. There are different versions, but in each the Indians are massacred and the Spaniards depart with the gold.

One legend indicates that the Caverna del Oro was used by the Spaniards to hide Aztec treasure carried north from

Mexico. Supposedly, the treasure was discovered by American Indians, and therein lies the reason for the conflict. There may be some truth to this story, because exploration of the cave has never indicated any presence of gold or of mining within the passageways of the Caverna del Oro.

In 1869 Elisha Horn presumably found the skeleton of a Spanish soldier clad in armor which had been pierced by an arrow. Some accounts indicate that the discovery was made on Horn Peak, nearly six miles north of Marble Mountain. Others locate the find at the Caverna del Oro. There is no proof to substantiate either.

The entrance to the Caverna del Oro is at an elevation of about 12,000 feet, above timberline, on Marble Mountain. Because of snow, the opening is inaccessible most of the year. During the time when entrance is obtainable, explorers must contend with wet passageways, ice, and strange wind currents throughout the cave. Many determined attempts have been made at exploration.

In 1880 J.H. Yoeman described a small fortress constructed of rock and timbers which was located adjacent to the entrance of a small cave further down the mountainside from the entrance to the Caverna del Oro. In 1920 Mrs. Apollina Apodaca, an elderly woman of Spanish descent, told the story that had been passed down through her family. She indicated that at a depth of 90 feet, Spaniards dug a horizontal tunnel in which Spanish gold was buried behind a set of padlocked doors.

Frederick G. Bonfils, co-founder of the *Denver Post*, financed an exploration of the Caverna del Oro in 1929. In one pit, a rusty iron chain ladder was discovered fastened to a heavy log which was wedged between the pit walls. Two expeditions were made into the cave in 1932. The first expedition discovered a skeleton with a metal strap around its neck -- as if a man had been chained by the neck and left to die. At a depth of 175 feet, the second expedition discovered crude wooden ladders which were constructed using wooden pins. Also located was a hammer -- its age dated to the 17th Century. The group found many Indian arrowheads at the little fortress further down the mountainside. The find added credence to the tales of conflicts between Spaniards and Indians.

As of this writing, the cave has been fairly well explored. No set of doors has ever been found. Could the tunnel (in which the gold was stored) have been mysteriously sealed? Did the Spaniards store their treasure in the cave and protect it from the fortress below? Did they remove all the gold before they abandoned the area? Or, is there still a treasure of riches hidden somewhere beneath the deep, dark passageways of the Caverna del Oro?

Scaling Long's Peak

BIRD ON A MOUNTAINTOP

Isabella Bird was an English lady, writer, and horsewoman who often rode country trails in her bloomers because she hated to ride side saddle -- the proper thing to do in those days. During one of her several trips to America she spent some time in the Rocky Mountains of Colorado, especially the high mountain valley nestled below 14,256 foot Long's Peak. Isabella was fascinated by one of the "residents", a scraggly mountain man named Jim Nugent, whose eye was missing and whose face was scarred as the result of an encounter with a grizzly bear. He loved to tell tall tales of trappers and Indians -- and she loved to listen.

Isabella had a zany idea that she wanted to climb Long's

Peak, the highest peak in the Estes Park area. One day in 1873, after urging Jim and two others to make the journey with her, they left with Isabella clad in a most unusual mountain climbing outfit. "It consisted of a half-fitting jacket, a skirt reaching to the ankles, and full Turkish trousers gathered with frills falling over the boots."

They climbed from crevice to crevice, clinging to narrow cracks in the rocky walls. They inched upwards, avoiding snowy and icy areas. Isabella was terrified, cold, and could hardly breathe and often begged Jim to leave her behind, but he would have none of it. For much of the climb, Jim had to drag her up "like a bale of goods by sheer force of muscle." At long last they reached the mountain top and her goal was achieved. In doing so Isabella Lucy Bird etched her name into the annals of Colorado history.

Waiting 'til Spring

SWINDLE AT PERU

Southwest of Argentine Pass, above the trail to Horseshoe Basin, was a place called Peru -- the site of a clever swindle. Silver was discovered along Peru Creek in the late 1860s. Claim owners who wanted no part of the harsh winter ahead, hired Gassy Thompson and his partner to dig and shore a tunnel one hundred feet long at their claim site. The owners informed Gassy that they would return in the spring to inspect his construction and pay him for his work. Timbers were hauled in, and Gassy and his partner began work.

As winter snows fell heavily and the miners encountered solid hard rock, Gassy suddenly had a "better" idea which would make their work easy and still earn their pay. Instead of digging into the mountain, Gassy began building snow sheds which "tunneled" out from the mountain. They timbered a full one hundred feet out from the face of the mountain. Heavy snow banked against the mountain completely covering the false tunnel until only its new entrance was visible. Meanwhile, Gassy and his partner spent a comfortable winter in the mine bunkhouse.

In April, while snow was still piled heavily over the tunnel, Gassy announced that his work was completed. As they had promised to do, the owners snowshoed up to the project to inspect the work. The delighted owners complimented Gassy and his partner on their formidable job -- and paid them in full.

The winter had been exceptionally severe, and it wasn't until July that the snow melted enough to expose the new timbers of the useless tunnel. The astonished mine owners were wroth with indignation. A search was begun for Gassy Thompson, but by this time he and his partner were long gone.

California Gulch

LEADVILLE: HOW IT HAPPENED

While prospecting in California Gulch on April 26, 1860, Abe Lee discovered gold and proclaimed, "Boys, I've got all California here in this pan." The stampede was on. Thousands of fortune seekers swarmed into California Gulch and the surrounding mountains. Tents and wagons were scattered from one end of the gulch to the other.

Initially, Lee and his group staked nearly the entire California Gulch with "speculative claims" in an effort to grab all of the property which might be potentially profitable. The plan didn't work, however, for new prospectors demanded a miners' meeting from which came the official "Bylaws of California Mining District, California Gulch, Arkansas River."

117

They were adopted on May 12, 1860, and established provisions as to the number, size and type of claims which could be filed. Fair laws invited more newcomers. By mid-summer there were 5,000 people scattered throughout California Gulch. Finally some order began to appear. Tents began to "colonize." The original site of Oro City, the largest camp, was located on the south edge of present day Leadville. More permanent structures replaced the temporary ones. It wasn't long before the camp had about 8,000 inhabitants.

Among the earliest arrivals into the region that spring, were Horace Austin Warner Tabor and his wife Augusta. H.A.W. Tabor, who was to become a pillar in the development of Leadville, arrived into California Gulch during a food shortage. He sacrificed his oxen so that hungry miners could eat, and by doing so immediately became the friend of many. Augusta established a little store where she sold her baked goods and provided meals as well. Like most of the men, Horace prospected the surrounding hills.

California Gulch yielded over $5,000,000 in gold during the next five years. By 1866, most of the placer gold was gone. The heavy black sand was hard to work and good accessible ore was difficult to obtain. Many prospectors became discouraged and moved on.

Charles J. Mullen and Cooper Smith, who were grubstaked by a Philadelphian named J. Marshall Paul, found a new rich lode at the Printer Boy Mine, and a new flurry of activity began. The Printer Boy was the first underground gold mine in the Leadville area and marked the transition from surface mining to underground hard rock mining. The remaining inhabitants of Oro City dismantled their cabins and moved them, along with their furnishings, up the gulch to the new location of Oro City, commonly called "Slabtown." New hotels, saloons, and stores sprang up.

The heavy black sand continued to make gold mining difficult. In 1875 William Stevens and Alvinus Wood decided to have the sand assayed. They discovered that it contained fifteen ounces of silver per ton and was rich in carbonate. They kept their find a secret for nearly two years. When the word spread in 1879, the silver boom was on.

Leadville was a simple community of log structures in 1878. By June of the following year, however, it had blossomed considerably. According to Cass Carpenter, as of May 1, 1879 Leadville had "... 19 hotels, 41 lodging houses, 82 drinking saloons, 38 restaurants, 13 wholesale liquor houses, 10 lumber yards, 7 smelting and reduction works, 2 sampling works for testing ores, 12 blacksmith shops, 6 livery stables, 6 jewelry stores, 3 undertakers, and 21 gambling houses where all sorts of games are played as openly as the Sunday School sermon is conducted." Additionally, there were 36 brothels. As George E. King and other architects arrived, the community took on an air of elegance and sophistication. This was something Leadville's many "suburbs" never had.

In 1876 the Adelaide Mine was located in Stray Horse Gulch. The town of Adelaide grew up in the flat valley near the mine of the same name. Although Adelaide was only two miles from Leadville and the route looked like one continuous town, the "suburb" had its own identity. The town had a post office, school, large smelter, and twenty-eight commercial buildings which included several saloons and stores. By 1879 Adelaide had a population of about 1,000. In addition to the Adelaide Mine, the Eureka, Humboldt, and Morning Glory all produced well.

A short distance above Adelaide was the location of the famous Little Jonny (which was recorded without the h) and the other Ibex mines. The Little Jonny made fortunes for John Campion and J.J. Brown. The Ibex Camp served the several properties of the Ibex Mining Company.

Finntown was situated between Leadville and Adelaide. Its population was predominantly Finnish -- hence the name.

The road up Little Stray Horse Gulch leads to the site where the small community of Evansville once existed, and on to Stumptown. Stumptown (originally named Stumpftown for Joseph Stumpf) is very similar to most of Leadville's "suburbs." Mines sprinkled the area east of Leadville like pepper from a pepper shaker. Wherever there was a cluster of mines, a camp usually sprang up, and some were very close together. Such was the case with Stumptown. Stumptown had several saloons and other businesses -- the most renowned being an always crowded pool hall, where betting was usually heavy. Among the many productive mines in the vicinity were the St. Louis, Louise, Winnie, Ollie Reed, Favorite, and the Miner Boy. In the 1890s a squabble broke out around the St. Louis Tunnel. The Miner Boy and the Colorado Prince had a dispute which wound up in violence. Both mines were burned. Cooler heads finally prevailed, and the claims were consolidated and worked by the St. Louis Tunnel.

South of Leadville stretched a group of "suburbs" once known as "Smelter Valley." Jacktown (which had a bowling alley), Stringtown, Bucktown, and Little Chicago (across the river) were blue-collar towns. In sharp contrast to some of the Victorian gingerbread in Leadville, Stringtown and its neighbors were comprised of many tenement shacks and plain cabins mixed with a few commercial buildings. The many chimneys at the smelting furnaces revealed their main source of prosperity. The giant Arkansas Valley Plant, a lead smelter, sprawled out between Stringtown and Bucktown. Most of Stringtown's residents were Arkansas Valley workers, as were those of Bucktown and Little Chicago. Founded in 1879 as the Billing and Eilers Smelter, the Arkansas Valley Plant was operated by the American Smelting & Refining Company. Several other smelters operated in the vicinity. Stringtown had a hotel -- the

120

Great Northern. There were many saloons, and cribs occupied by girls of the night -- and day. The valley was a tough place, with fights and violence commonplace.

Millionaires were made. In May 1878, Horace Tabor grubstaked August Rische and George Hook to $17 worth of supplies for a third interest in their findings. He added another $47 worth of tools to the grubstake. Rische and Hook discovered the Little Pittsburg (often spelled Pittsburgh) Mine and made Tabor an instant millionaire. Tabor once purchased a "salted mine", the Chrysolite, but instead of considering it a bad deal, he further developed the property and struck rich silver ore. Later, Tabor purchased the Matchless Mine for $117,000 -- possibly the only investment he made without partners. During the peak years of its operation, the Matchless yielded $1,000,000 per year. Two of the area's successful mines, the Minnie, and the A.Y. helped spring Meyer Guggenheim on his way to a fortune. The mines enabled Swiss-born Guggenheim to compile much wealth which he spread into other mining endeavors. He invested into the smelting industry and other properties in which his seven sons all became millionaires as well. David May opened the Great Western Auction House and Clothing Store in Leadville on January 1, 1878. This was the forerunner of the department store chain known today as the May Company. The successful hardware store of Charles Boettcher was the foundation for another fortune. Boettcher moved his holdings to Denver and amassed extraordinary wealth. James Viola Dexter was another man made rich by Leadville silver. Samuel Newhouse eventually became a copper magnate after he struck it rich in Leadville. The Morning Star Mine added to the riches of two-time governor John L. Routt. The wealthy John F. Campion later developed the beet sugar industry in Colorado. Jack McCombe became a wealthy man off the Maid of Erin Mine. He spent much of his wealth, however, sending expensive presents to everyone he knew in Ireland, his home country. Yes, many millionaires were made. And the list goes on -- and on.

In 1878 prospectors, merchants, and others trickled into town from all directions. Dr. David H. Dougan closed his office in Alma, crossed Mosquito Pass, and set up shop in Leadville. Nobody seemed to need a doctor, however, and Dougan sat in his office for 28 days without a patient. On the 29th day he received word that there had been a mine accident and he was needed immediately. That was the beginning of his illustrious career in Leadville. Dougan was a successful physician, then became mayor in 1881, and later was president of the Carbonate National Bank.

As previously mentioned, Leadville was once a village of log structures. George Albert Harris built the first log hotel on Chestnut Street in May of 1877. On January 14, 1878, the community was officially named. Beginning with the boom of 1879, the growth of Leadville was rapid. Harrison Avenue emerged as the center of the business community where most of the hotels, banks and restaurants were located. Horace Tabor, who became mayor in 1878, built both the Clarendon Hotel and the elegant Tabor Opera House the following year. Many important people and famous stars graced the stage of the Tabor Opera House. Lectures were held by British critic and poet, Oscar Wilde. Wilde raised a few eyebrows by drinking several Leadville miners under the table. Central City's Jack Langrishe and his players performed for the more cultured. The great Harry Houdini performed his magic on stage. Shakespearian actor Laurence Barrett appeared with his supporting cast. Boxing matches were held headlined by prizefighters John L. Sullivan and James Corbett. Sousa's Marine Band was among many to appear at the facility. The elaborate Tabor Grand Hotel, with silver dollars set into its lobby floor, was opened in 1885.

Soapy Smith learned the principles of the old shell game in Leadville. Col. William F. Cody, "Buffalo Bill", came to town with his Wild West Show. Famous gunfighter and gambler, Doc Holliday, made at least two visits to the community. Prostitute and storyteller, Laura Evans, spent about three wild years in Leadville. During a tour of mining camps in 1877, Susan B. Anthony stopped in town to lecture for woman's suffrage. Several men of the cloth left their mark as well, including Father John Dyer, Father Macheboeuf (who made annual visits to California Gulch in the early days), Pastor Arthur Lake, Father Robinson, and the Reverend Tom A. Uzzell.

Leadville also had its seedy side. Most of the many saloons, gambling dens, dance halls, and brothels were located along State Street and in its dingy corridors. There was Tiger Alley, French Row, Coon Row, and Stillborn Alley. It was one of the most wicked and rowdy areas in the entire old west. There were elegant bordellos and one-girl cribs. Many of the dance halls and saloons had rooms above where more than just a garter was removed. Tough men, painted women, and slick gamblers could be found at "joints" such as the Bucket of Blood, the Pioneer, the aptly named Red Light Hall, the Carbonate Concert Hall, the National, the Odeon, the Bon Ton, the Bella Union, and the Little Casino. Madams such as Mollie Price, Mollie May and Sallie Purple ran "houses" which catered to a fairly respectable clientele. In contrast, the cribs had girls of every size and shape, and every color and origin, and would cater to anyone. Top prostitutes such as the Pioneer's sassy Maude Deuel could make as much as $200 per week. The Texas House, which was located on the corner of State Street and Harrison Avenue, was one of the largest gambling halls in Colorado. Many fortunes were made in Leadville -- and a part of many were spent on State Street.

Many of the Carbonate Kings lost their fortunes in 1893. President Cleveland repealed the Sherman Silver Purchase Act whereby the government would no longer purchase silver to back its currency. The foreign market for silver collapsed as well. Leadville was dealt a crippling blow, but it wasn't about to die.

And, that is how it happened.

Mine guard

THE PELICAN AND DIVES' FEUD

Ill, and seemingly on his death-bed, Owen Feenan confidently advised two friends of a rich strike located in Cherokee Gulch. One which he had been keeping a secret. Feenan recuperated to find that his "Pelican Mine" was being worked, and that his "friends" had excluded him from the operation. A camp nearby called Silver Plume also had sprung into existence during his absence. Feenan realized no reward for his rich find. The Pelican lived through a plague of troubles to become one of the area's most successful mines.

Speculation that the Pelican and Dives mines were tapping the same vein created a feud which wound up in litigation. Twenty-three separate suits were on file at one time contesting rights to the rich eight-foot silver vein. Pelican owners believed that the Dives' management was stealing their ore. On one occasion, an accident supposedly claimed six lives. Coffins were lowered into the mine, then raised and hurried away. The accident was a hoax -- the coffins contained high-grade ore. Armed guards were hired and stationed at both mining properties. Tensions mounted and both sides braced for a full-blown war.

Jacob Snyder, one of the Pelican's owners, left the mine one morning in 1875 and departed for Georgetown. En route he was accosted by Jack Bishop, a Dives lessee. Bishop followed Snyder to the edge of town, overtook him at the livery stable, and struck him with his pistol. He then fatally shot Snyder through the head.

After the murder, Bishop fled to Empire to seek out his friend Harry Carns who lived at the brewery of Paul Lindstrom. Bishop told Carns that a posse was close behind and asked to be hidden. Carns led the fugitive into a dark cellar and hid him behind some large brewing vats. His horse had been hidden in a nearby thicket. When the sheriff arrived, he asked Carns if he had seen Bishop. Carns answered with a little chuckle, "Sure, he's hiding behind old man Lindstrom's beer kegs. Go in and look for him." The sheriff didn't believe Carns, and rode off with the posse. Paul Lindstrom's wife furnished Carns with food and blankets but was not given a reason for the supplies. Several months later Mrs. Lindstrom received an envelope containing money but no letter or note. She had assumed the food and blankets were for Jack Bishop -- and now she was certain that the money had been sent by him as payment and thanks.

The feud over the eight-foot silver vein became so intense that during the hearings Judge Belford was forced to keep loaded pistols on the bench. Massive amounts of money were spent on litigation. Following the death of the Dives' J. H. McMurdy, the conflict began to subside. The two mining properties were ultimately purchased by magnate William A. Hamill, of Georgetown, and consolidated as the Pelican-Dives. Hamill who had purchased the Dives for $50,000 at a sheriff's sale, sold the combined properties in 1880 for $5,000,000 to become one of the richest men in the region.

"Hello Sheriff!"

FOILED FLIGHT

In 1898 Harry Tracy, formerly a member of Butch Cassidy's gang, and his partner David Lant were arrested for the murder of a deputy. They were taken to Hahns Peak, Colorado and locked up in a unique jail to await trial. The Hahns Peak jail was called the "Bear Cage" because it was literally a welded box of bars.

Hahns Peak had a tough and determined sheriff named Charles Neiman. One night, Tracy and Lant tricked and overpowered Neiman and escaped leaving the badly beaten and unconscious sheriff behind. They felt certain that Neiman would be "out" for a long time allowing them to make good their escape. They stole two horses and rode out of Hahns Peak.

The resilient Sheriff Neiman regained consciousness and set out after the escapees. Realizing the fugitives were not dressed for the weather, the sheriff was certain they would try to hold up the Hot Sulfur Springs stagecoach. Neiman and a deputy boarded the stage in Hahns Peak with the hope that his prediction would be correct. Lo and behold, several hours later the stage was held up. When they opened the stage door, the astonished Tracy and Lant were looking down the barrels of two shotguns. The fugitives were returned to the "Bear Cage." This time the two decided to sleep days in order to spend their nights hollering, screaming, and generally making all the noise they could so as to keep the townspeople awake. It worked -- within days they were transferred to the Pitkin County jail in Aspen. Once again they escaped after almost beating a guard to death.

David Lant disappeared. Some say he was killed by Tracy, but there seems to be no evidence to substantiate that claim. Harry Tracy, whose hideout for awhile was in the Muddy Creek area north of Wolcott, became even more notorious. He was jailed in Oregon -- and escaped. He died near Davenport, Washington in 1902. Wounded, and with a posse in pursuit, Tracy shot himself to death to avoid being taken alive.

Alferd Packer

CANNIBAL PACKER

In 1874, at the foot of Slumgullion Pass, the remains of five men were discovered. One had been shot, the other four had their skulls crushed. Each of the bodies had been carved up and fleshy parts removed. Herein lies the legend of Alferd Packer - that part of history for which Lake City is most famous. The bizarre story of Packer's gruesome escapades has been told and retold. By some, so graphically that blood literally drips from the written word. The grim tale is told here in such a way as to minimize the unpleasantries.

Alferd Packer was a member of a prospecting party which departed from Salt Lake City, Utah, in November 1873, bound for the mountains of Colorado. Late in the month of January

131

1874, the party of miners arrived at the encampment of Chief Ouray and his tribe of Utes, near the confluence of the Uncompahgre and Gunnison rivers. The weather had been severe and snows were deep. Chief Ouray advised the miners that they should not continue on their trek until spring. After remaining with the Utes for nearly three weeks, Packer and five others were convinced they could proceed on. They left the Utes, and the others in their prospecting party, to continue their journey.

More than two months later, Packer arrived alone at the Los Pinos Indian Agency near Saguache. Here he told General Adams and others how he had lost his companions in a snowstorm. He identified the lost miners as Israel Swan, George Noon, Frank Miller, James Humphreys, and Wilson Bell.

Some time later, more members of the original prospecting party arrived at the Los Pinos Agency. After being advised of the plight of Alferd Packer, a fellow named Lutzenheiser suggested to General Adams that foul play might be involved. He indicated that Packer (who had been spending money freely at Los Pinos) had earlier been nearly broke, and furthermore that Packer's Winchester rifle possibly belonged to Israel Swan. With everyone's suspicions aroused, Packer was ordered to accompany a search party for the missing five.

Shortly thereafter, an Indian found some human flesh on the trail used by Packer. With the discovery of this new evidence, Packer unraveled a dreadful new story. According to Packer, starvation was close at hand, so Swan was killed by the others and they ate his flesh. Within a few days Humphreys died and he also became a meal. Packer claimed that Noon and Bell killed Miller, and that days later Bell shot Noon. Packer stated that Bell attempted to kill him, and that he had to kill Bell in self defense. Packer admitted to living off the others' flesh in order to survive. Packer was jailed pending a further investigation.

Near the banks of the Lake Fork of the Gunnison River, at the foot of Slumgullion Pass, five partially decomposed bodies were found in August 1874. It was evident that the men had been murdered and cannibalized. By the time word of the horrid discovery had reached Saguache, Packer had escaped from jail and disappeared. Alferd Packer fled to Wyoming, and lived under an assumed name. Nine years later he was recognized, captured, and returned to Lake City, Colorado. On April 13, 1883, Judge Melville B. Gerry found Packer guilty of the murder of Israel Swan, and sentenced him to death by hanging.

It was the first, and possibly only incident of cannibalism tried in the United States court system. When sentence was pronounced, according to legend and poet Stella Pavich, the judge told Packer that, "...There was siven Dimmycrats in Hinsdale County! But you, yah voracious, man-eatin son of a b____, Yah et five of them, therefore I sentence ye T' be hanged by the neck ontil y're dead, dead, dead!" The comical and often-repeated quotation was not really a statement from Judge M.B. Gerry, an articulate gentleman.

In actuality, the eloquent and sophisticated Judge Gerry made the following statement to Packer before pronouncing sentence, "You and your victims had had a weary march, and when the shadows of the mountain fell upon your little party and night drew her sable curtain around you, your unsuspecting victims lay down on the ground and were soon lost in the sleep of the weary; and when thus sweetly unconscious of any danger from any quarter and particularly from you, their trusted companion, you cruelly and brutally slew them all. Whether your murderous hand was guided by the misty light of the moon, or the flickering blaze of the campfire, you only can tell. No eye saw the bloody deed performed; no ear save your own caught the groans of your dying victims. You then and there robbed the living life and then you robbed the dead of the reward of the honest toil which they had accumulated ..."

Alferd Packer was awarded a retrial on a technicality. In 1886, at the retrial in Gunnison, Packer was found guilty of manslaughter and sent to prison in Canon City. Before he left office in 1901, Governor Charles S. Thomas pardoned Alferd Packer. Newswoman, Polly Pry, who had crusaded for his release, was instrumental in getting Packer a job as doorman at the *Denver Post*. In 1907 Alferd Packer was laid to rest in the cemetery at Littleton, Colorado beneath the tombstone which misspelled his first name. A commemorative to the five victims lies at the foot of Slumgullion Pass. Isn't it strange that the site where Alferd Packer allegedly had his meals is named after a miner's stew -- slumgullion?

The Old Homestead

RED LIGHTS OF MYERS AVENUE

Cripple Creek was dubbed "the world's greatest gold camp." Its mining district was the fifth largest single gold producing area in the world. The total gold production for the district has been estimated at a half-billion dollars. Cripple Creek has been called, "the last great boom town." And boom it did -- as mines worked three shifts in a twenty four hour period; hotels were jammed to capacity; and some boarding houses rented cots by "shifts." The town was literally packed with people. And because of it, Cripple Creek had a full-blown, non-stop, wild and boisterous red-light district.

It all started in 1890 when Bob Womack discovered gold in Poverty Gulch. Horace Bennett and Julius Myers promptly

135

platted a town and sold lots. The two main streets were named for themselves, and the town of Cripple Creek was established.

Bennett Avenue was lined with hotels, department stores, specialty shops, doctors' offices, and many other kinds of businesses. The stock exchange and half of the banks in the district were on Bennett Avenue. It was the center of high-finance. Most of the "low" finance took place on Myers Avenue. Parlor houses, cribs, gambling dens, dance halls, and many saloons lined the street which became one of the most notorious in the West.

The earliest buildings on Myers Avenue, as well as the rest of Cripple Creek, were mostly frame construction -- and they weren't to last long. On April 25, 1896, a fire broke out on Myers Avenue when dance hall girl Jennie Larue and her bartender boyfriend knocked over a stove while quarreling. Aided by a strong wind, it swept through the lower end of town, destroying about one third of the business district in just four hours. Just four days later, on April 29th, a second fire which began at the Portland Hotel engulfed most of what remained. The two fires left thousands homeless and destroyed over $2,000,000 worth of property. Help came from far and wide -- and construction began immediately to build a "new" Cripple Creek predominantly of brick and stone.

Myers Avenue re-emerged with a carnival-like atmosphere. The Bon Ton and other variety theaters had three or four piece bands playing out front in order to attract customers to their establishments. The Old Homestead at 353 Myers Avenue was a posh bordello with crystal chandeliers, wallpaper from Paris, Oriental carpets, stoves in every room, and it even had bathrooms. Madam Pearl DeVere threw elegant champagne parties for the exclusive clientele at the Old Homestead. Other fancy houses on Myers Avenue were the Royal Inn, the Boston, Neil McClusky's, and Laura Bell's. Myers Avenue tailed out into Poverty Gulch where most of the one-girl cribs were located. Most of the cribs were small two-room shanties. Customers were solicited by the girls at their front doors. The night life in Cripple Creek was -- to put it mildly -- wild! This could be attested by a tombstone in Mt. Pisgah cemetery bearing the inscription, "He called Bill Smith a liar." The largest gambling hall was Johnny Nolan's at 3rd Street and Bennett Avenue. The Last Chance, the Miner's Exchange, the Opera Club and the Dawson Club were a few of the seventy three saloons in Cripple Creek at the turn of the century. A shooting, one night, at the Dawson Club was reported by the *Cripple Creek Times* as follows:

> "An inquest was held at Lampman's morgue today over the body of James S. F. Roberts who was shot last night at the Dawson Club on Myers Avenue. Thirteen witnesses testified. They were comprised of girls of the half-world, the Dawson Club piano player, the bartender and members of the police force. One of the witnesses said that as the man lay on the floor dying some of the crowd urged him to the bar for a drink."

Three hundred prostitutes operated in Cripple Creek, and for the most part they did so with little trouble from the police. Those places known to be opium dens had more trouble with the law. There were a few in the alleys which paralleled Myers Avenue, and a few more down in Poverty Gulch. One account states:

> "Another opium den was raided yesterday. The police, for several days, have been watching the apartment of Lizzie Moore. Yesterday, the captain noticed three women go there at 6:00 a.m. After a quarter of an hour, the captain tiptoed in to the find the women and the proprietress reclining on a Turkish rug, hitting the pipe."

Julian Street, the author, visited Cripple Creek to write a story about the gold camp for *Collier's*. When the article was published, to the chagrin of Cripple Creek's fathers, he described the community as, "the most awful little city in the world." The debasing account dwelled on Myers Avenue. Citizens were so disgusted that shortly thereafter a city ordinance officially changed the name of Myers Avenue to "Julian Street."

There was an element of culture on Myers Avenue. Across the street from the Old Homestead stood the Grand Opera House. Many famous performers of the day graced its stage. The Grand Opera House was used for operas, plays, sporting events, political rallies, and other attractions.

For years, Myers Avenue ran wide open -- and then it didn't. Life in the red-light district is one of the most colorful chapters in the city's history. Cripple Creek endured.

"Scabs" fell to their death at the Independence Mine

THE VICTOR LABOR WARS

Victor's history was one of fortune and misfortune -- in a very plural sense. Gold and glitter were mixed with tension and tragedy.

Winfield Scott Stratton's Independence Mine was the most celebrated in the district. The Portland had the greatest yield, but the Ajax also produced well. On the edge of town was the Strong Mine, another top moneymaker. Battle Mountain, where these four mines were located, produced over $125,000,000 worth of gold making it one of the richest spots on earth.

The Florence and Cripple Creek Railroad arrived in Victor in 1894, followed by the Midland Terminal Railroad the next year. The Colorado Springs and Cripple Creek District Railroad (commonly called the Short Line) arrived a few years later. There were two trolley lines -- the High Line and the Low Line. Trains and trolley cars passed through Victor every few minutes. The city, with its mines and railroads, was the industrial center of the Cripple Creek Mining District.

Victor, its neighboring communities and nearby mines, was the scene of two violent labor wars. In 1894, union officials failed in their efforts to establish a uniform wage throughout the vicinity. The union wanted $3.00 per day for eight hours of work. The mine owners ignored the union's request. A strike was called by the Western Federation of Miners, picket lines were established, and trouble began. Several skirmishes occurred before Governor Davis H. Waite was called in as an arbitrator. He settled the strike and established a standard wage of $3.00 for an eight hour day, which is what the union wanted in the first place.

The Western Federation of Miners called a second strike in 1903 to protest the firing of two men for their union activities in nearby Colorado Springs. Owners reopened the mines with heavily guarded non-union scabs. During the ensuing violence, two mine officials were killed near the town of Independence in an explosion at the Vindicator Mine, a train carrying non-union persons was wrecked, and fifteen scabs fell to their death because someone had tampered with the cable to an elevator car at the Independence Mine.

Colorado had a new governor who sympathized with the mine owners. Governor James Peabody sent in the Colorado National Guard and established a state of martial law. After six months of occupation and relative quiet, troops were withdrawn.

Once again violence erupted. On June 6, 1904, twenty-five non-union workers from the night shift at the Findlay Mine were waiting at the Independence depot for the train to take them home, when a bomb exploded under the depot's platform.

Thirteen scabs were killed and many others injured. [Note: The explosion at the Independence depot was later attributed to union strong-arm Harry Orchard.]

On the following day mine owners took things into their own hands. They forced the sheriff to resign and appointed one of their own men to replace him. All of the mines were ordered closed -- and the saloons, as well. Two more men were killed when a riot broke out in Victor. The militia was called in again. This time union people were shipped out of the area by rail to Kansas and New Mexico with orders not to return. The troops were withdrawn on July 26, 1904.

The Mine Owner's Association instituted a card system of employment and reopened the mines. "Approved" applicants for work received a card which allowed them to be employed. A worker's card was retained by his employer while he was on the job. Trouble makers had their cards withheld and could not obtain work at any of the area's mines. The labor wars were over, but the scars were indelible.

Prunes

PRUNES, A BURRO

On Front Street in Fairplay, stands a memorial to the burro, Prunes. The inscription on the face of the monument reads: "Prunes, a burro; 1867-1930; Fairplay, Alma, all mines in this district."

Prunes was a friend of the community and faithful companion to prospector Rupert Sherwood. They worked side-by-side, and they are buried side-by-side.

A burro was a prospector's best friend. The sturdy, hardworking little animal had amazing strength. Not only would he carry a prospector's ax, pick-ax, shovel, frying pan, groceries, bed roll, and other supplies, but he would carry heavy bags of ore from the mine to the mill. He could haul timbers or iron rails. Or, his strength could be harnessed to move large rocks. A prospector would be "lost" without his burro.

Prunes and Rupe worked together for years throughout the Mosquito Mining District. Rupe would spend his cold winters in Denver leaving Prunes in Fairplay to be cared for by the townspeople. They became very attached to the lovable little animal.

Rupe and Prunes grew old together. Eventually Prunes became very ill and had to be taken out of his misery.

Money was collected from the townspeople of Fairplay and Alma (for they both claimed him), to build a monument in his memory.

A year later Rupe Sherwood became seriously ill. Before he died, he requested that his body be buried next to his faithful pal -- and his wish was granted.

*   *   *   *   *   *   *

[Note: The inscription on Prunes' memorial reads 1867-1930, indicating that he lived 63 years. According to several reliable sources the life expectancy of a burro is between 10 and 25 years (35 years in captivity). It is highly unlikely that Prunes lived the years indicated on the inscription.]

He felt very despondent

POOR JAMES FENTON

There is a common belief among fortune hunters. Each man believes that he will be the one to find the "pot at the end of the rainbow." The quest to strike it rich has not only fueled a million dreams, but it has driven man to the limits of his physical capacity and to the brink of insanity. Such was the case with James Fenton.

Fenton suffered from a severe case of rheumatoid arthritis. The chronic disease caused him great pain and discomfort for years. The ache in his joints and muscles was often agonizing, and his hands showed a degree of deformity. His dreams, however, spurred him on.

Thousands flocked to Leadville during the silver boom of

1879. James Fenton was one of the easterners who joined the throng. The town, which a year earlier consisted of simple log structures, suddenly blossomed into 19 hotels, 41 lodging houses, 82 saloons, 38 restaurants, and many other buildings. Fenton prospected the hills east of Leadville before moving down to Lake Park where he constructed a log cabin. He worked one claim after another but barely eked out a subsidence.

One day, while working his twelfth claim, Fenton felt very despondent. He was probably suffering from a combination of his rheumatoid arthritis and his continuing mining failures. He had been blasting and was down to his last stick of dynamite. He carefully placed the charge above one of the timbers which shored his tunnel -- and lit it. He moved a few steps away, lay down on his back and folded his arms across his chest.

When rescuers finally uncovered his body and saw the position in which he was lying, they realized that his death was no accident. Poor James Fenton departed from this world without finding the "pot at the end of the rainbow," but in so doing his painful ailments departed as well.

Nathan C. Meeker

THE MEEKER MASSACRE

The Ute Indian nation consisted of many tribes. Most were peaceful. The great Chief Ouray fell heir to the Uncompahgre tribe at age 17. He was a man of great vision who could speak both English and Spanish. Through his unparalleled strength of character and artful negotiations, Chief Ouray was more responsible than any other person for gaining peace between the Indian and white man in Colorado. Most of the Utes adhered to Ouray's wisdom, but some of the chiefs believed they had been pushed too far and took matters into their own hands.

In 1878 at age 60, Nathan C. Meeker became the Indian agent at the White River Agency. Meeker, who was heavily in debt, sought the job in order to repay his loans. He, his wife

Arvilla, and one daughter Josephine left their Greeley home and relocated at White River.

Meeker's plans for the Indians were a disaster. He envisioned converting the Ute from his nomadic life to that of a farmer. He totally failed to understand the ways of the Indian. He imposed his policies until the Utes could take no more.

September 30, 1879, was the fateful day of the "Meeker Massacre." Ute braves raided the White River Agency. Nathan Meeker was killed and mutilated. Ten of his employees were also massacred. The Indians took all of the guns and supplies, then burned the buildings. Arvilla Meeker, Josephine, and three others were taken as hostages. During the time they were captive, Josephine received better treatment than the others. She had operated a school for Ute children at the agency, knew and understood the Indians' problems, and even took their side in many disagreements which they had had with her father. Arvilla and Josephine eventually returned to Greeley.

More than any other single event, the Meeker Massacre spelled doom for the Utes in Colorado. Legislation was passed, and a new treaty was signed which actually "paid" the Ute Indians to move further west to their new home in Utah.

Justice shall be served!

GOOD GUYS AND BAD GUYS

On the Argentine Road, nearly 3 miles east of the Montezuma Road, lies the site where the little mining town of Chihuahua once existed. The life of Chihuahua was short lived. The settlement was incorporated in 1880 and destroyed by a forest fire in 1889. During the interim, it boomed. There were two hotels -- the Chihuahua and the Snively, a sawmill, a reduction works, several stores, and a small "community" schoolhouse east of town which it shared with its neighbor Decatur (later to become Argentine).

Chihuahua had no doctor or preacher. The residents boasted that none were needed, so the story goes, because there wasn't any sickness or sin.

A tale is told about two Chihuahua prospectors (the good guys) who were waylaid by several rogues (the bad guys). The prospectors were robbed and killed. Residents quickly heard of the tragedy, formed a posse, and went after the killers. The undeputized posse of townsfolk chased the fugitives up the trail around Copper Mountain. Three of the rogues were caught high on Ruby Mountain. Chihuahua had no judge -- nor did it have a jail. Suitable "hanging" trees were found for the occasion, and the culprits were immediately lynched. All five bodies were carried back to town.

Somewhere near Chihuahua there are two gravesites -- one for the good guys and one for the bad guys. The preacher who wasn't needed in this "sinless" town, wasn't there to give last rites.

A strange man hovered over his daughter's bed

BACHELOR'S SAD STORY

Fortune seekers flocked to Bachelor Mountain by the hundreds during the winter of 1891-92, after the Last Chance Mine struck paydirt. The bustling and rowdy boom town of Bachelor sprang to life. Following the construction of a boardinghouse, the next three "businesses" built were two saloons and a parlor house -- a reflection of the wild nature of the community. Shootings, accidents, and fires were common occurrences during the town's short life. One murder involves an unusual cast of characters. It is a sad story indeed.

Winters were cold in the high-mountain community of Bachelor which was situated at an elevation of 10,526 feet. Snow would pile high, and sometimes the wind-chill would became unbearable. One winter the small daughter of the town's minister became dangerously ill with pneumonia. He knew that she needed medical help, but no doctor lived in Bachelor. So, the minister decided to fight the adverse weather and travel to nearby Creede with the hope that he could fetch a doctor.

Upon returning home, he found a strange man hovering over his daughter's bed. Thinking the man was up to no good, he killed him on the spot. After learning the man was a doctor attempting to help his daughter, the minister was distraught and committed suicide. His daughter also died of her illness.

A gravesite located below Bachelor in a grove of aspen is said to contain the bodies of the minister, his daughter and the doctor. Supposedly they are buried one on top of the other because of the difficulty of digging graves in the frozen ground of winter.

Jerome B. Wheeler

ASPEN, THE EARLY YEARS

The Leadville silver boom was such a bonanza that prospectors spread out hoping to find similar success elsewhere. During the summer of 1879, claims were staked on Aspen Mountain, West Aspen Mountain and Smuggler Mountain. By the spring of 1880, the rush to the Roaring Fork Valley was on.

Henry B. Gillespie was one of the first settlers. He purchased a few of the earliest claims and established a camp which he called Ute City. Gillespie had big plans for Ute City, but as snow set in he left for the winter. B. Clark Wheeler was more impatient, however, and challenged the snow. He had Ute City surveyed. Wheeler renamed the settlement Aspen and, with the assistance of David Hyman and others, they platted an

153

addition to the original townsite. The community was a crude mix of log cabins, frame structures, and many, many tents. The "business district" consisted of a hotel, restaurant, assay office, a few stores and other businesses, and several saloons.

The first road to Aspen came from Buena Vista across Taylor Pass and through the town of Ashcroft. Aspen became more accessible when Independence Pass from Twin Lakes and Leadville opened in late 1881. The three factors which contributed most to the early success of the town were the rich silver mines, financier Jerome B. Wheeler (no relation to Clark), and the railroads.

Some of the best early mines were the Durant, Smuggler, Spar, Mollie Gibson, Aspen, and the Castle. H. P. Cowenhoven, a merchant who would grubstake most any prospector, acquired a share of the Aspen Mine in settlement of a $400 debt. The mine made a fortune for Cowenhoven and his son-in-law David R. C. Brown. A prospector once sold a half interest in the Smuggler Mine for a burro and $50. The Smuggler produced millions, including the largest silver nugget in the world. Ore from the Mollie Gibson assayed at 3,300 ounces of silver per ton. The Durant, which was purchased by David Hyman, ran into the Aspen claim and wound up in litigation. The result was a compromise which made all parties rich. The Aspen was once leased by J. D. Hooper who made a rich strike shortly before the expiration of his lease. During the final days he extracted $600,000 worth of ore. Henry Tourtelotte (for whom Tourtelotte Park is named) located the Castle and several other lodes. Other top producers were the Midnight, Newman, Lone Pine, Washington, Consolidated, Argentum-Juniata, Park Regent, Montezuma, Free Silver, Bush Wacker, Vallejo, and the Emma. One small chamber in the Emma netted $500,000. The Lone Pine consolidated with the Mollie Gibson to form the Compromise Mining Company. The largest body of silver ore in the world found to date was located in 1883 in the

Compromise Mine. During the same year, a new rich deposit was discovered in the Spar Mine.

Jerome B. Wheeler, a large stockholder in Macy's department store (New York), and the Colorado Midland Railroad among other things, arrived in the Roaring Fork Valley in 1883. He invested much money into Aspen and encouraged others to do likewise. The first electric tramway ever constructed for mining purposes was built by Wheeler. It carried ores from the Aspen Mine, down Aspen Mountain into the valley. In 1884 Jerome Wheeler built a smelter at the mouth of Castle Creek, and ores could be treated locally. Wheeler and Henry Gillespie built a mill and concentrator, and expanded underground exploration at the Mollie Gibson Mine. His investments and contributions were not always mining-related. He established and edited a newspaper, the *Aspen Daily Times*, and backed the construction of both the Hotel Jerome and Wheeler Grand Opera House. Both structures were impressive, and cost $1,000,000 each. The three-story hotel was lavish. Its furnishings were imported from overseas. The hotel had electricity, a barber shop, billiard parlor, and an elaborate dining hall. The opening Grand Ball in 1889 was a celebration of most luxurious splendor. The Opera House boasted exquisite ornamental woodwork with brass trimmings as well as plush upholstery and curtains. Wheeler was also instrumental in bringing the Colorado Midland Railroad to Aspen.

A spur of the Denver & Rio Grande narrow gauge reached Aspen from Glenwood Springs in November 1887. The Colorado Midland, a standard gauge, arrived the following year from Leadville -- through the newly constructed Hagerman Tunnel (which cost $2,000,000). A confrontation occurred between the two railroads which nearly wound up in gunfire. Mayor Henry Webber stepped in, and a peaceful solution emerged. Each railroad built separate depots and did so on opposite sides of town. They both shipped ore successfully for

155

many years.

The arrival of the railroads boosted mining, which in-turn increased population. Mining output in 1888 exceeded $7,000,000, approximately double what it was in 1884. By 1889 it had reached nearly $10,000,000. Likewise, Aspen's population was 3,500 in 1884. Following the coming of the railroad, its population expanded to 8,000 in 1888. The increase continued, and by 1892 the population had reached 12,000 and Aspen was the third largest city in the state. By then it had surpassed Leadville to become the world's greatest silver mining camp.

The crude little settlement of the early 1880s blossomed into a well-established city. It grew as a refined city -- with class. Much of its exceptional society can be attributed to the quality and character of Aspen's forefathers. From the early years on, there were many churches, cultural activities, socials, fraternal organizations, and civic clubs which projected for Aspen a much better image than that of most mining towns.

From February 1881 when Aspen was designated as the temporary county seat of newly created Pitkin County, politics has had its place. Soon after construction began on the new Pitkin County Courthouse in July 1890, controversy arose amid newspaper reports of bond fraud and misappropriations by county commissioners. Regardless, it was completed in January 1891. It is one of the oldest courthouses in Colorado still used as such. Davis Hanson Waite settled in Aspen in 1881 and launched the *Aspen Union Era*, a weekly newspaper which championed reform and Populist ideas. He was elected Governor of Colorado on the Populist ticket in 1892. After the silver crash in 1893, Waite received the nickname "Bloody Bridles" and became embroiled in controversy following his speech, " ... for it is better, infinitely better, that blood should flow to the horses' bridles rather than our national liberties should be destroyed ... " (*Rocky Mountain News*, July 12, 1893).

In addition to Waite's weekly newspaper there were at least two other weeklies and three dailies -- the *Aspen Times* (*Aspen Daily Times*), a fine newspaper which was once purchased by Waite, then sold to B. Clark Wheeler (who later became his son-in-law); the *Rocky Mountain Sun*; and the *Evening Chronicle*.

By 1892 Aspen was a bustling city with electric lights and telephone service. Ten passenger trains arrived and departed daily. There were horse-drawn street cars. The Hotel Jerome was the finest of many hotels and boardinghouses. Besides the Wheeler Opera House, another popular spot was the Rink Opera House. Aspen had ten churches, three banks, a hospital, three schools, and even a racetrack. There were government buildings such as Armory Hall (National Guard) and the aforementioned Pitkin County Courthouse. Additionally, the business district was full of stores and specialty shops (such as the Kobey Shoe and Clothing Company and Reide's City Bakery). As with most every mining town, there were dance halls, gambling dens, and saloons, the majority of which lined Cooper Street. They were supplied by Aspen's own brewery. Part of Durant Street was a "red light district." Many brothels housed the ladies of the night (and day). The city taxed each girl $5 per month. On weekends, large crowds would gather to watch Aspen's semi-pro baseball team take on teams from Denver, Leadville, and other cities. Homes throughout Aspen displayed much diversity. There was a multitude of miner's cottages, but there were also many stately houses -- elegant examples of Queen Anne architecture.

The silver crash in 1893 had a devastating affect on Aspen. Within one month after the devaluation, all area mines had shut down. Economic strife hit the community. Some millionaires had diversified their interests enough to stay afloat -- others went bankrupt. After the price of silver stabilized, some of the mines reopened. The economy wouldn't rebound however.

Aspen's population dwindled -- and continued to do so. By 1930 the community had 700 residents.

During World War II, ski troops of the 87th Mountain Infantry (which later became part of the 10th Mountain Division) trained on slopes near Aspen. Several of the members loved Aspen and returned after the war to establish skiing. Walter Paepcke (head of the Container Corporation of America) envisioned an opportunity, and poured investment capital into the community and the ski industry. Aspen today booms as it did over 100 years ago and is a world class ski resort.

Cleveholm

JOHN OSGOOD'S UTOPIA

John Cleveland Osgood had a unique philosophy of industrial relations -- particularly those which involved the relationship between employer and employee. He believed that the employer's role should carry beyond the work place to the employee's standard of life. He knew that if his workers were well cared for off the job they would be happy, and it would reflect in their performance on the job. Alongside the Crystal River, he created his ideal industrial community -- his utopia -- Redstone.

Osgood founded the Colorado Fuel Company, purchased the Colorado Coal & Iron Company, and then merged the two to form the Colorado Fuel & Iron Company. The coal empire of the CF&I operated mines at nearby Coal Basin for many years. A narrow-gauge railroad transported the coal, down a grade that sometimes exceeded four percent, to the coke ovens at Redstone for carbonization. Osgood controlled CF&I for just one decade, but it was during this time that Redstone was built.

Redstone was a company town. Only employees who worked in the coal mines nearby, at the coke ovens across the river, or in another capacity for Osgood were permitted to reside in the community. On tree-shaded lots, stood unique, pastel-colored homes which were provided for workers with families. The tudor-style Redstone Inn was constructed as a clubhouse for Osgood's workers and a residence for the unmarried men. The inn contained elegant furnishings, a bar, pool tables, and a piano. There was also a library and a theater for employees and their families. The village was dubbed, "The Ruby of the Rockies."

Beyond the village -- and beyond the massive wrought iron gates -- stands the magnificent 42-room mansion "Cleveholm." Osgood constructed his splendid English tudor manor house beside the Crystal River on 450 acres of land. It can still be seen in all its beauty. Some of the ceilings are gold-leafed. Oak wall panels were stenciled by Italian artists. A fireplace of hand-cut stone is the focal point of the drawing room. The library walls are adorned with hand-tooled green leather and elephant hide. The dining room is decorated in ruby velvet, and the music room in green silk brocade. Osgood imported many of the furnishings from throughout the world. Cleveholm was constructed at a cost of $2,500,000.

Osgood had three wives -- each of which created her own share of gossip. His first wife wrote steamy novels about their marriage. The life of his second had been touched with scandal. Because of her generosity, however, she was dubbed "Lady Bountiful." Osgood's third wife -- who eventually sold Cleveholm after his death -- was fifty years younger than he.

John Osgood died in 1926, at age 75. His utopian community Redstone remains as a memorial to his originality, his benevolence, and his vision.

Raisin' a ruckus!

EAT, DRINK AND BE MERRY

Perhaps there should have been a sign at the town limits which read, "While in Arrow - Eat, Drink and be Merry." It doesn't seem as though the town had too much else to offer. Arrow (originally called Arrowhead) began as a railroad construction camp (in 1904) high on the road to Rollins Pass.

Restaurants in small mountain towns sometimes left a lot to be desired. Such was the case with Jack Graham's place -- a saloon and restaurant. There were no menus. Customers paid 25 cents for a tin plate and cup. The tin plate was used for whatever food Graham happened to be serving. The cup was provided so a customer could draw from the barrel of water if a drink other than booze was desired.

Adjacent to the Denver & Salt Lake Railroad depot was a sign on the wall which read "Dining Room." The official name of this establishment was the Denver Railroad News and Hotel Company Eating House. Another business place with a rather descriptive name was the Furnished Rooms Establishment. The Chancey De Puy Hotel was a fancy name for a not-so-elaborate hotel. During its short life, Arrow also had a couple of other hotels, a few stores, sixteen saloons, a livery stable, and a "red-light" district where parlor houses and gambling dens operated side-by-side. There was never a church -- though it was certainly needed. The little town of about 200 inhabitants "swelled" considerably on weekends. Many miners and railroad workers flocked in to pick up their mail and spend a "hot" Saturday night at the "establishments."

An old-fashioned western ruckus stirred up in September 1906. Neil Ragland was the town constable. He also "owned and operated" some of the "sporting" girls in town. Indian Tom Reynolds was a half-breed who drank heavily and couldn't take a joke. One of Ragland's girls hid $20 of Indian Tom's money behind a picture and wouldn't tell him where it was. The incensed and drunken half-breed went on a rampage. He rode his pinto into Jack Graham's place and sprayed bullets everywhere. The harassments continued the following evening until it was all Neil Ragland could take. He lay low in the shadows of the darkened Elk Saloon knowing the Indian would soon arrive. When Indian Tom entered the bar -- Ragland shot him through the heart. Well, some merriment sours.

The community was economically troubled from the outset. It was greatly overbuilt and the rate of business failure was high. It seems as though its main objective for existing was to provide a place to "eat, drink, and be merry." Within two short years, most of the residents had packed up and moved on.

High tailin' it!

THE ILL-FATED JIM REYNOLDS GANG

Jim Reynolds was one of the early settlers at the little South Park camp of Fairplay. When the Civil War broke out, Jim and his brother John headed south to join the army of the Confederate States of America. The financial structure of the Confederacy was unstable from the beginning and further weakened as the war progressed. Word spread near and far of all the new-found riches in Colorado -- some of which might help the Confederate cause if it could be diverted to the South. The adventurous Jim Reynolds, accompanied by his brother John and seven other rebels, rode into Colorado bent on highjacking as much gold as possible to aid the Confederacy. Some say that these intentions were just a ploy -- that the Reynolds Gang planned only to make themselves rich.

Jim Reynolds and his gang left an obvious trail through South Park. Everyone seemed to know where they were and that they were moving toward Denver. After a lucrative stagecoach robbery, the gang rode east along the South Platte River. They eluded one posse, but a larger one was in pursuit.

The gang made camp near Deer Creek, while Jim and John Reynolds carried the loot to a safe hiding place. Shortly thereafter, the posse was able to sneak up on the gang. One of Reynolds' men was fatally shot, but the rest escaped. Later, Jim Reynolds and four other gang members were captured near Canon City. John Reynolds and two others escaped to New Mexico.

Jim Reynolds and the other four prisoners were tried in Denver for highway robbery and sentenced to the prison at Fort Leavenworth. During the trip to the prison, the five men were shot to death.

In 1871, while dying from a bullet wound, John Reynolds told a friend where the stolen loot was hidden. The friend was never able to find the loot -- nor has anyone else -- and many have tried over the years. Estimates as to the value of the stash vary from a pittance to quite a treasure. Who knows -- but somewhere in the fifteen-mile expanse between Handcart Gulch and Elk Creek, the stolen loot may possibly remain buried.

Mrs. J.J. Brown

THE UNSINKABLE MRS. BROWN

Margaret Tobin was born in Hannibal, Missouri, on July 19, 1867. She was the fourth of six children born to Irish immigrant John Tobin. Maggie, as she was known in her earlier years, grew up in Hannibal -- but she couldn't wait to leave. Mary Ann Landrigan, Maggie's half-sister, moved to Leadville in 1883, during the silver boom. Maggie was working as a waitress at Hannibal's Park Hotel when Mary Ann beckoned. It was all the encouragement Maggie needed. She and her elder brother Daniel packed their suitcases and boarded a train bound for Leadville.

It wasn't long before Maggie met James J. Brown. Maggie had always dreamed of marrying a rich man. J.J. Brown wasn't rich, but he was bright, determined and "had promise." J.J. was an aspiring superintendent of the Louisville Mine -- while Maggie was a sales clerk at the emporium of Daniels, Fisher and Smith. On September 2, 1886, at age 19, Margaret Tobin married J.J. Brown.

J.J. Brown became a minor stockholder in John F. Campion's Little Jonny Mine. After the silver crash in 1893, Brown devised a method to tunnel through sand, and tapped vast quantities of high-grade gold. His ingenuity was rewarded with 12,500 shares of stock. Production in 1894 was so high that the company paid dividends of one million dollars. J.J. and Maggie were rich.

J.J., Maggie, and their two children, Lawrence and Helen, moved to their new Denver mansion at 1340 Pennsylvania Street, on prestigious Capitol Hill. Maggie moved in the circles of Denver society, but could not crack the elite Sacred 36. The small exclusive group simply thought that Mrs. Brown lacked an element of refinement and culture. Over the next several years, Maggie became a world traveler, social climber, philanthropist, heroine, and even had aspirations for political office. Her jewels and elegant wardrobe were as fine as money could buy. She hobnobbed with nobility. Maggie learned to speak several languages and traveled with the international set. Following one of her voyages home from Europe in 1912, Mrs. J..J. Brown became an international celebrity.

Maggie, or Molly as she had become known to Denverites, booked passage from Cherbourg to New York on the maiden voyage of the Titanic. Nearly five days into the voyage, the ship which was thought to be unsinkable, struck an iceberg. Slowly, in the cold of night, the great Titanic began sinking into the sea. The passengers and crew totaled 2,228. Less than one-third survived. Mrs. Brown escaped the catastrophe in lifeboat number six.

Maggie loved to embellish the truth, and it certainly helped as she took on the role of heroine. Maggie stated, "It is true that I was at the oars for five hours, but really, why call me a heroine? I believe that whatever we do is more or less selfish. I rowed to keep away from the suction when the Titanic went down; I rowed to reach the boat whose light we saw later; I rowed to reach the Carpathia. You see it was selfish, wasn't it?" Her expensive chinchilla coat covered three children -- as she joked, and sang songs to keep her boatload of survivors awake and active in the cold of night. Once aboard the rescue ship, she spent her time caring for the injured survivors.

Upon her arrival back in Denver, Maggie was quickly accepted into the exclusive Sacred 36. Now a woman of international stature, the society that once shunned her, now welcomed her with open arms.

Maggie loved to talk -- and now the world was listening. When asked how she accomplished what she did, her reply was, "Typical Brown luck. I'm unsinkable." A legend was born. Years after her death in 1932, Margaret Tobin Brown was assured immortality when her life story was portrayed on stage and screen in *The Unsinkable Molly Brown*.

Acknowledgements

Sincere appreciation goes out to my mother, Ruth S. Bennett, and Teresa Bond. Their long hours and dedication helped make this book possible.

I am also grateful to Richard L. Southworth, Luther E. Bennett, Jeani Speciale, Joel Sommers, Nancy Flanders, Hal Flanders, Ray B. Walling, John Haney and Doreen Wollmer for their proof-reading and suggestions.

Additionally, I extend my thanks to the Colorado Historical Society and the Denver Public Library, Western History Department, for photographs used to help depict some of the likenesses portrayed in this book's illustrations.

Dave Southworth

Bibliography

BOOKS

Bancroft, Caroline. *Augusta Tabor: Her Side of the Scandal.* Boulder: Johnson Publishing Co., 1955.

Bancroft, Caroline. *Colorado's Lost Gold Mines and Buried Treasure.* Boulder: Johnson Publishing Co., 1961.

Bancroft, Caroline. *Silver Queen: The Fabulous Story of Baby Doe Tabor.* Boulder: Johnson Publishing Co., 1955.

Bates, Margaret. *A Quick History of Lake City, Colorado.* Colorado Springs: Little London Press, 1973.

Benham, Jack L. *Camp Bird and the Revenue.* Ouray: Bear Creek Publishing Co., 1980.

Bishop, Isabella Bird. *A Lady's Life in the Rocky Mountains.* Norman: University of Oklahoma Press, 1960.

Blair, Edward. *Everybody Came to Leadville.* Leadville: Timberline Books, 1971.

Blair, Edward. *Leadville: Colorado's Magic City.* Boulder: Pruett Publishing Company, 1980.

Bruyen, Kathleen. *"Aunt" Clara Brown, Story of a Black Pioneer.* Boulder: Pruett Publishing Company, 1970.

Bueler, Gladys R. *Colorado's Colorful Characters.* Boulder: Pruett Publishing Co., 1981.

Byers, William N. *Encyclopedia of Biography of Colorado.* Chicago: Century Publishing and Engraving Co., 1901.

Crofutt, George A. *Crofutt's Grip-Sack Guide of Colorado.* Boulder: Johnson Books, 1885.

Dallas, Sandra. *Colorado Ghost Towns and Mining Camps.* Norman: University of Oklahoma Press, 1985.

Dallas, Sandra. *Gaslights and Gingerbread.* Athens, OH: Swallow Press, 1965.

Dyer, J. L. *Snow-shoe Itinerant.* Cincinnati: Cranston & Stowe, 1890. Reprinted Breckenridge: Father Dyer United Methodist Church, 1975.

Eberhart, Perry. *Guide to the Colorado Ghost Towns and Mining Camps.* Denver: Sage Books, 1968.

Ellis, Amanda M. *Pioneers.* Colorado Springs: Dentan Publishing, 1955.

Fay, Abbott. *Famous Coloradans.* Ronia: Mountaintop Books, 1990.

Feitz, Leland. *Soapy Smith's Creede.* Colorado Springs: Little London Press, 1973.

Fossett, Frank. *Colorado.* New York: C.G. Crawford, 1880.

Griswold, Don L. and Griswold, Jean H. *The Carbonate Camp Called Leadville.* Denver: University of Denver, 1951.

Hall, Frank. *History of the State of Colorado. 4 Vols.* Chicago: Blakely Printing Co., 1889, 1890, 1891, 1895.

Harrison, Louise C. *Empire and the Berthoud Pass.* Denver: Big Mountain Press, 1964.

Hollenback, Frank R. *Central City and Black Hawk*. Denver: Sage Books, 1961.

Jessen, Kenneth. *Eccentric Colorado*. Boulder: Pruett Publishing Company, 1985.

McLean, Evalyn Walsh. *Father Struck It Rich*. Boston: Little, Brown and Co., 1936.

Monnett, John H. *Colorado Profiles: Men and Women Who Shaped the Centennial State*. Evergreen: Cordillera Press, 1987.

Stevenson, Thelma V. *Historic Hahns Peak*. Fort Collins: Robinson Press, 1979.

U.S. Bureau of the Census, Revised by the Social Science Research Council. *The Statistical History of the United States from Colonial Times to the Present*. Stanford: Fairfield Publishers, Inc., 1965.

Voynick, Stephen M. *The Making of a Hardrock Miner*. Berkeley: Howell-North, 1978.

Wolle, Muriel Sibell. *Stampede to Timberline*. Denver: Sage Books, 1962.

Wright, Carolyn and Clarence. *Tiny Hinsdale of the Silvery San Juans*. Denver: Big Mountain Press, 1964.

NEWSPAPERS

Breckenridge Bulletin

Carbonate Chronicle

Central City Daily

Central City Register-Call

Courant (Idaho Springs)

ado Prospector (Denver)

Creede Candle

Cripple Creek Gold Rush

Cripple Creek Times

Denver Post

Denver Republican

Denver Times

Denver Tribune

Fairplay Flume

Georgetown Courier

Herald Democrat (Leadville)

Lake City Mining Register

LaPlata Miner

Miner (Silverton)

Mineral County Miner (Creede)

Ouray Herald

Ouray Times

Republican (Telluride)

Rico Weekly Sun

Rocky Mountain News

San Juan Herald

Silver World (Lake City)

Silverton Democrat

Silverton Standard

Solid Muldoon (Ouray)

Summit County Leader (Breckenridge)

Telluride Journal

ARTICLES

Halaas, David Fridtjof and Gerald C. Morton. "Boom and Bust: Images from the Colorado Chronicle." *Colorado Heritage.* Colorado Historical Society. (Issues 1 & 2, 1983).

Harvey, Mrs. James R. "The Leadville Ice Palace of 1896." *Colorado Magazine* 17, No. 3 (May, 1940):94-101.

James, Louise Boyd. "The Case of the Colorado Cannibal or `Have a Friend for Dinner'." *American West.* (February 1990).

Smith, Duane A. and David Fridtjof Halaas. "A Fifty-Niner Miner: The Career of Horace W. Tabor." *Colorado Heritage.* Colorado Historical Society. (Issues 1 & 2, 1983).

OTHER SOURCES

Leadville Mining District compiled from official records and other reliable sources, January 1901, Charles F. Saunders. Also copyright 1901 by Charles F. Saunders.

United States Geological Survey, Maps, U.S. Department of the Interior, Federal Center, Denver.

Thayer's Map of Colorado Published by H. L. Thayer,

Denver, Col., 1880. From Surveys of the General Land Office, used by permission, revised and corrected to date by the Publisher.

First Annual Colorado Mining Directory, 1896. Compiled by J. S. Bartow and P. A. Simmons. Denver: The Colorado Mining Directory Co.